Friend, Foe, or Family

by

Deborah Tilson Clark

To Terry:

without you, nothing

Published by Human Error Publishing
Paul Richmond
www.humanerrorpublishing.com
paul@humanerrorpublishing.com

ISBN:
978-0-9973472-2-7

Illustrations and cover art by Jessie Tilson Clark

List of Stories

Be Not Afraid of My Greatness

"...be not afraid of my greatness; some are born great, some achieve greatness, and some have greatness thrust upon them." -- William Shakespeare, *Twelfth Night,* Act II, Scene 5

Yeah. And some of us are doomed to be the sidekick, the deputy who never gets to be sheriff, the star's girlfriend whose throat gets cut by Freddie Kruger in the first scene. Where's the greatness those characters deserved? When do they get their fair share of the fortune and glory?

I'm always interested in the underdog, and yes, it is for the obvious reason. I am a mutt. But I'll tell you what, old Will Shakes-His-Spear, I am not afraid of anyone's greatness and especially not those who think they are born that way.

Right now, while Mrs. Decauter is re-filling her stainless steel, guaranteed-to-keep-it-hot-for-hours coffee mug from the pot in the teachers' lounge, I am going to pick up the three literature books that have been left in the floor. I will also pick up the crumpled sheet of notebook paper from where Cody dropped it, and the test paper that not two minutes ago I returned to Rachelle, who promptly stuck it in her notebook where it lingered just long enough to be carried to the shelves, then slipped out and into the floor. It won't really matter, though, because the grade has been accurately and legibly entered into the hard copy gradebook – by guess who – so when Rachelle's mother, the elementary school teacher, checks into why her cheerleading daughter has only a lowly C average for the six weeks, we can point to the evidence. It's a cinch Mrs. Decauter wouldn't be able to explain it, because she barely knows who Rachelle is, much less the fact that Rachelle has been skipping Fridays for three weeks now, going with her boyfriend for long rides in the boyfriend's new Mustang, and missing those regular vocab quizzes without bothering to make them up.

I know, because I grade the papers, I check the homework, and I am the one who listens to what the kids are telling each other. God knows they never tell the old battleaxe anything, not even the answers to the questions she asks at the end of every chapter of every book she's assigned for the ten thousandth time. Doesn't she realize the students pass around copies of quizzes and tests that she's used for the past eon? They don't even charge each other for them, any more.

Isn't she even suspicious about why her department gives in so easily, every year, to her teaching all the upperclassmen honors classes? Senior honors kids are generally smart enough to take no serious harm from her worthless teaching, and they all bring home straight A's because they're using her old assessments to go by. So Momma and kids are all satisfied and Mrs. All-Star Teacher gets to be a hardass on the tardy and no-hats-in-the-school rules (like they mattered). Duh.

What really gripes me is when some snob parent says, "Oh, Mrs. Decauter is the best teacher in the high school. She's old style and she's strict, and the students learn to buckle down and behave, in her classroom."

Get a clue.

"To endure is greater than to dare; to tire out hostile forces, to be daunted by no difficulty, to keep heart when all have lost it – who can say this is not part of greatness?" --William Makepeace Thackeray

"Shirley, did you get those reports graded last night?"

Mrs. Decauter stands with one hand wrapped around her coffee mug, the other flipping idly through the pages of her grade book. She doesn't even know where to look to see if the grades have been entered. But all her nails are perfectly enameled, and her lipstick matches, and her hair is beautifully dyed. She's wearing a nicely fitted "casual-professional" outfit of tailored dark grey slacks, silky white blouse, and a boxy jacket that looks like it has been made out of upholstery material. Today she even has on pointy-toed, high-heeled shoes, rather inappropriate for someone her age, I should think, and possible for her only because she sits down all day, every day. No aching feet for that old trout.

"Yes. The grades are in the book, behind the green tab. I was just about to hand them out."

"I'll take a look at them first," she says, and sticks her hand out.

I walk over and hand her the stack of papers, but I know she won't read them. They're hand-written, and she won't take the time to decipher the squiggles and curves that the kids pass off for hand-writing, these days. I go over and mark the attendance in the book, keeping an eye on her while I'm at it. Sure enough, I see her stare at the paper on top of the stack, frown, then lift it to see the next one, and the next, and the next. In a few seconds she lays the whole stack down on her desk and walks to the front of the room. I move discreetly to the back of the room, get the papers, and start handing them out, whispering to each kid what he's done well or poorly, what grammar mistake he's making too often, why his grade is high or low.

"Class," she announces, "we're going to try something a little different, for a while."

We are? This is a shocker, coming from the woman whose last original thought was in 1962, when she told Johnny Musser he looked like one of the Beau Brummels. (In a small town like this, there are no secrets.)

"For the remainder of this six weeks, I want us to begin each class meeting with a responsive writing."

Now I get it. Lucille, who cleans the floors, said she heard the principal, Mr. Bales, telling Mr. King that he wants all the teachers in the English Department to do this start-up writing thing. So this is not a new thought for Mrs. D. Thank God. I'd hate to have to clean up the mess from her head exploding, if she ever really did think up something new on her own.

So she goes on to give a too-short but too-wordy explanation of what the kids are supposed to do, and I go around the room, translating that into understandable instructions: reserve space in your notebook, respond to a brief prompt, three hundred words, blah blah blah. You'd think she'd notice that I know what to tell the kids before she's even through making her pronouncement, but no, she probably doesn't even see me anymore. I'm just here, part of the furniture.

My god, she probably believes I sleep in the janitor's closet at night, like I used to think my second grade teacher did. Like I have no life outside this building.

So today the kids are supposed to write "a brief autobiographical statement about themselves" (Should somebody remind her what "autobiography" means?) and starting tomorrow, there will be a quote on the SmartBoard for them to respond to as soon as they get into their seats.

I'd bet my next paycheck I already know who gets to come up with a quote every day.

Yep. Even as I stand here, she's informing me that I should have the next day's quote typed in and ready to go, before I leave to go home. And maybe I should develop a theme for each week.

Right. Okay-dokey, Mrs. D. I'll get to it right after I grade all the papers I collected from the students today, and after I lay out your lesson plans for tomorrow – after all, it is a little too much to ask that you go through your previous year's plans and figure out which one comes next, and lay it out where you can see it first thing in the morning, or where Mr. Bales can see it, if he should come snooping around for a quick, unannounced observation.

Maybe I should leave a big turd on your desk, too, Mrs. D.

"It is necessary to be slightly underemployed if you are to do something significant." -- James Watson

I used to think doing this – being an aide - was better than being a janitor. That's how I got into the business, so to speak. My second husband's sister, Shawnna, got on at the middle school, and she talked me into trying for the job at the high school, when it came open.

"Shirl, you should apply. You might get it, and I tell you, it's not hard. Nobody really pays any attention to what you get done, you know?"

"I don't know, Shawnna. I'd just rather stay on at Lincoln. No offense, but cleaning up after a bunch of kids seems like it would get boring. At least at the factory, I can try to make production. Maybe I could even get on as shift supervisor. There's some chance of advancing."

"Are you kidding? When's the last time you heard of anybody off the floor moving up to supervisor? And you know they're sending all the work to Jamaica or Mexico or some place where the people will work for a quarter an hour."

I couldn't argue with that. There were less than half as many people working at the building I was in, where we finished the jeans and denim skirts and jumpers that have made our brand famous in trendy mall stores, than there were a year ago. Less than half.

That's what made me fill out the application for the custodial position at the high school. It was a pay cut, especially considering the extra I always pulled in for making production despite them raising the amount nearly every month, and I took some guff for that, from friends and especially from my husband. Eighteen months later, though, Lincoln Fashion Works was closed and Shawnna's brother, soon to be my ex-husband, was living with his girlfriend and I was grateful for that steady paycheck and guess what, Shawnna had been right about another thing, too: nobody paid any attention to what I did or didn't do, during my shift at school.

It was weird, being back in that school. Ours was the first class to graduate from the "new" building, back in 1978. We thought it was the spiffiest, shiniest, best thing in the world. We were proud to be Gullion Gladiators, like knowing all the words to the fight song would help us pay the mortgages on the double-wides we bought as soon as we got on at Lincoln. When I first started working here, though, I wasn't so proud to be back. I hid my face from everyone in the halls. Glenna Royall was a math teacher back when I was a student, and her husband, Jimmy, coached and was paid to teach social studies, although the only things his students have ever learned from him was how to draw lines on the football field with powdered lime. Both of them are still in the trenches at GHS. Mr. Bales, who'd been assistant principal when I was in school, advanced to being the principal, and he settled in there in the leather chair with rollers and armrests, and is waiting for retirement to meet him. And one of my classmates, Jenny Bickerton, is teaching in the science department. But most of them just ignore me; maybe they do not recognize me, or they simply don't see me, or they are actually being snooty. Who knows. If they ever wonder why the girl who walked these halls as an honors student is now cleaning the floors, they never bother to ask.

Anyway, it was probably my pride as much as the minuscule raise I would get, that made me apply for the aide position. After four years of working in maintenance, I thought it would be nice not to have to pick up trash and deal with rude teenagers. And so what am I doing now? Picking up trash and dealing with rude teenagers AND doing all of Mrs. Decater's work besides.

"There are no great men, only great challenges that ordinary men are forced by circumstances to meet." -- William F. Halsey

As soon as the final bell rings, I ask Mrs. Decauter if she can stay with the students to whom she has assigned fifth period for tardies. Surely, for once, she can sit with the students that she's made stay after school for minor rules infractions. She loves assigning fifth periods; it is one way she maintains her "old school discipline" reputation, and she never has to suffer the consequences. I stay with the kids and she sails out the door with her expensive, too-big handbag over her shoulder, on her way, no doubt, to a swim and a massage at the Wellness Center followed by fourteen hours of sleep on her Memory Comfort mattress.

So I tell her I need to prepare the paperwork for her next day's classes and before she can think up a reason she can't stay the extra 15 minutes, I head to the media center to run copies of tomorrow's handouts. Two kids catch me on the way, and start wailing about how they can't find books they can possibly get through in time to do a book-in-a-bag report next week, and could I please help them find something fun and short and also on Mrs. D's list? By the time I get them settled, and help the new aide for the Science Department make copies for her teachers, and run all the copies Mrs. D's students will need, it's nearly four o'clock and I know Mrs. D and her little delinquents are long gone. Peace reigneth in GHS, and I decide to use the quiet and Bartlett's Familiar Quotations to get the quotes for next week's start-up assignments. The subject of work is tempting, but would the kids have anything to say about that?

I am reading over my list as I enter the classroom, one set of copied handouts dangling over my arm and a second set riding crosswise to them. I look up to see that a miracle of the first water has occurred: Mrs. MaryBeth Simpson Decauter is still in her classroom, more than an hour after the dismissal bell has rung. I stop, and I am a little miffed that the old patootie has actually done something worthwhile for a change. Not only am I used to her doing everything halfway, but when she does, I have free reign and good cause to gripe about her and compare myself most favorably to her. Because she's such a train wreck, I appear to steam along pretty well. Or at least, I can tell myself that I do.

"I have a list of quotes for next week's start-up assignments," I say. She's leaning forward over her desk, left elbow planted firmly on top of the ENG III Lit teacher's guide, cheek propped on her wrist. She's turned a little away from me, so I can't see her face. I realize she is dozing.

Ha, I think. I might have known she wasn't actually doing any work.

"I have the quotes for next week," I say, a little more loudly than the first time.

Still no answer. No acknowledgement at all. I step closer and say, quite loudly, "Mrs. Decauter!"

"Mrs. Decauter?"

Even before I touch her shoulder – I have never before, not in the three years I've been her classroom aide, touched this woman – I know. Mrs. Decauter is dead. I stand there for a few seconds, too stunned to think. Then I reach over and make sure. Her skin is cool. Her face has a gray tone, making her rouge, brushed in long oblongs below her eyes, stand out like a smeared Raggedy Ann's.

Tacky, Mrs. D., I think. Meaning the rouge.

Come to think of it, keeling over after work hours on the desk she'd drummed with her fingertips about ten million times wasn't so cool, either.

I stand there for a minute, looking at the hair on the back of Mrs. D's head, noticing that it is Perfectly Auburn to the skin, and how someone had shaved the back of her neck right up to the oh-so-evenly trimmed edge that gently curls toward her chin. The collar of the expensive jacket gapes a little, exposing the tag of the beautiful blouse. It reads "Yves St Laurent." Even I – the ex-jeans seamer -- know that name. I remember when I learned it's pro-nounced "Eeves," not "Yee-vees," the way I'd said it in my mind when I'd read the articles in the fashion magazines my daughter carried home. Before she died.

"Some great people are leaders and others are more lucky, in the right place at the right time." -- Steve Wozniak

It is the tag that does it. Before that, I'd had no thought, abso-lutely no idea, of doing anything sneaky to poor old Mrs. D. That tag reminds me of DeAnna, who'd loved to read about fashion and designers and runway models, and who killed herself trying to be skinny enough to have a chance at modeling, and no one, not one teacher or guidance counselor or school friend, had noticed until it was too late.

I hadn't noticed, either. I was too busy working three jobs, trying to make the payments on that trailer after I'd left her sack-of-shit father, to pay attention to the too-large clothes. I was never there at mealtime to see if she ate, much less to fix a real meal for her. Even now I can barely admit that it might have been the way I pushed her to do good, to study hard and dress nice and stay away from most of her classmates, to just do everything not the way I had done it, the way that landed me pregnant and then married to a jerk and then working at Lincoln, that contributed to her anorexia. Oh yes, there was plenty of guilt to go around.

The pain of losing my daughter, the agony of admitting my part in her death, is still, years later, enough to make my gut cramp and my vision shrink. I have to lean forward a little, there at Mrs. Decauter's desk with her cooling carcass still propped on her un-callused hand, to let it pass, before I can breathe again.

And at that moment, with Mrs. D's designer blouse tag taunting me, something just clicks in my spine and I straighten up and start figuring things out.

First of all, what would be the normal thing to do in this situation? Call people: call the family, the funeral home, the rescue squad, the police.

Mrs. Decuter had no family that I knew of. Her father was long dead, mother gone years ago. No children. The police?

It occurs to me that someone might have… Could Mrs. Decauter have been murdered? I look at the perfectly coiffured hair, the nice clothes, her zipped-up handbag sitting smugly in the floor near her right foot. I think of the halls that had emptied so quickly of every student and, a few minutes later, of all but a very few teachers. I consider the surveillance cameras positioned at every corner, the subject of endless discussion in the community since they'd cost a small fortune to install (grant money) and a "safety officer" had had to be hired to sit in a downstairs office, eat doughnuts, and watch the monitors all day (an on-going expense nobody had taken into account, when the decision to get into the film industry had been made).

Nah. The biddy died of meanness and over-consumption of everything nice.

Over-consumption. Except for the few months she'd stayed married to the younger college man she'd dragged home and probably scared to death in the bedroom, she'd lived alone her entire adult life, too stingy to share anything with anybody. Instead, she'd spent her good salary – the Master's Degree was an automatic ten percent raise, National Board Certification was another twelve percent; with the years she'd kept that chair warm, she'd been taking home twice… no, easily three times what I was being paid and spending it all – on herself. If I made that kind of money, you can bet I'd find something better than tapestry-weave designer jackets to spend it on.

I back up and sit in a student desk without taking my eyes off that jacket. She got the salary, but I did the work. I am a better teacher than she'd ever been, no question. I've been in all the other classrooms, I've seen what other teachers do that works. I listen to the kids and I know how they respond to assignments and lectures. I've read the entire Standard Course of Study for English, and I know what's BS in that erudite little (128 pages) document, and what it is that the Powers are really looking for (They want the kids to be able to communicate verbally and in writing, and to sound just like them when they do.) Best of all, I know and like the kids. I like being with young people, watching them discover who they are and what they believe in; I enjoy their craziness and their first-time-for-everything-ness. In a just world, I'd be teaching and winning awards for helping young people, instead of cleaning floors and covering up the messes of an inadequate fill-the-seat teacher who had metaphorically left the building years ago.

And now, to add insult to that old injury, the county would hire some little thing just out of college and pay her –- or him, oh my God – diddly (but still more than they pay me), and the newbie would know nothing about the subject because for four years all she'd done was study esoteric information about obscure authors and manuscripts un-read by any but the dissertationally challenged, and she would be run over by these students like a turtle going east-to-west on VA 55 at 5:15 pm on a Friday. God and everyone who's in the system (even the janitors) knows that colleges do not teach teaching in their Education classes.

The county would save money, and the students would suffer. Same old story. For the kind of money MaryBeth Decauter was making, I could… I'd pack knowledge into their nostrils with a spoon. I've been doing everything important connected to this classroom except collecting the big paycheck, for years.

Everything except collect the big paycheck.

I stand up and walk back to Mrs. Decauter's side. I look down at that big, black purse. After a few moments, I stick my foot out, snag one handle, and drag it to my side of the corpse. I don't even hesitate to open it up and poke around, and sure enough, there between her matching wallet and gold-initialed datebook is a pristine county-stamped envelope. I lift the un-glued flap, and there is her paycheck stub.

So, Mrs. Decauter had her paychecks direct-deposited. Without thinking about what I am doing, I reach into her purse and pull out the wallet. I push open the snap, glance at her driver's license, the pad of checks, the surprisingly few credit cards (and none of the grocery store "preferred customer" cards of which I have five. Did the woman never buy groceries? Or maybe she never cared about getting ten-percent off.). But there was a debit card. With a debit card, you don't have to sign receipts. But you do have to key in a pin number.

I look at the slot where Dacauter had kept her debit card, and a slip of paper is sticking up. Just a corner. I pull it out and there's the number: 0614. I can't resist checking it against her driver's license and sure enough, it's her birthdate, June 14. What an idiot.

Even if she didn't return to work next fall, this woman who would, without a doubt, have set up her payroll on a year-round schedule, would be paid for this month, April; and May, and then June, July and August, before someone would have to inform the Central Office that she would no longer be showing up at GHS. In that time, she'd be paid... more than I'd be paid for working all year.

I swear, even if it had been there, in that envelope, ready for anyone to sign and cash, I wouldn't actually have taken Mrs. Decauter's paycheck. Not at that moment. Or maybe I would have. But one thing I will admit: an idea had been planted in my mind.

If I was doing her work, shouldn't I...?

It is at this point that my thinking, that for a few minutes has been all mixed up, nothing but a chaotic blend of DeAnna and guilt, MaryBeth Decauter and anger, paychecks and justice, starts settling along two lines, two ways for this situation to end.

Two roads diverged, I thought. *And sorry I could not travel both/ And be one traveler, long I stood..."*

How many times had I stood at one side of the room while MaryBeth Decauter read that poem to a roomfull of 16-year-olds, and then informed them that Robert Frost was a folk poet whose work was limited to the rural experiences of an earlier era? Wouldn't she be shocked to learn that I love the poetry of Robert Frost and think he had lots of things to say that are applicable to today's world? Even this mess.

Which path would benefit the students? A month from the end of the semester, deep into their research papers and end-of-course test preparation, the last thing they need is to be put in the care of a substitute who doesn't know jack about the subject, much less be able to exert crowd control. A new-hire would be a disaster; what first-timer could keep the seniors' attention focused on their final projects instead prom, their class trip, and the summer ahead? I am the person who could keep them on track and on course, but the school wouldn't hire me as a sub, because I'm not certified. What would be best for the students would be for the administration to be kept oblivious of Mrs. Decauter's death, at least for a few weeks, so I could continue to do what I do well.

"I distrust Great Men. They produce a desert of uniformity around them and often a pool of blood too, and I always feel a little man's pleasure when they come a cropper." --E. M. Forster

The only hard part would be getting rid of the body. I could bury her, but I'd have to get her out of the building first, and there were all those cameras. Then I'd have to dig a hole deep enough: too much chance of someone noticing. Put her in a closet, or hide her anywhere, and soon she'd be stinking. I even make myself consider cutting her into bits, carrying her out one chunk at a time, and dropping the pieces into various trash cans around the county. A woman can carry loads of anything in those totes they hand out at teachers' conferences (Not that I'd ever gotten to go, but Mrs. Decauter had ALWAYS gone, carried home all the free stuff she could possibly get her hands on, and then handed the bags to me to unload and stash.) and nobody ever notices. But I can barely force myself to think about all that... cutting, much less actually do it.

In the end, I know that cremation is the only way that will work. I even know where to build the funeral pyre: the old furnace in the Ag Building.

They use the furnace to get rid of scraps from the Woods and Building classes, and to keep the shop warm enough for the boys to work in, in the winter. Vocational Education is so out of style now, the School Board keeps looking for reasons to shut down the program altogether, and the teachers over there suspect that a high heating bill would be one of if not the final nail in their particular coffin. So they leave the thermostats turned off and burn available materials and keep turning out boys who know how to lay block and brick, hammer joists together and figure building supplies, and keep the county's fleet of ten-year-old cars running. I'd noticed smoke coming from the chimney during the cold snap of the last week. I know the furnace door opens easily – I'd burned enough paper trash and cardboard boxes in there, while I was in Maintenance – and I know it is big enough to take MaryBeth Decauter entire. I only have to figure out how to get her from her desk to the shop without going in front of the surveillance cameras.

It is easy, really. She is already sitting in the rolling desk chair. I walk down the hall to the janitor's closet, get one of the giant-sized, super-strength plastic garbage bags – cleaning up after hours was something I did so routinely, I knew that it would be no cause for suspicion if anybody happened to check the film of Friday-after-hours -- and slip it over her head and body, right down to her fancy high-heeled shoes. But not under the casters. Rolling her to the window is a cinch, and the gathering darkness is a plus.

As I push her out the window, her body obligingly slumps itself into the big black bag. It is the only cooperative thing she's done in years. Too bad nobody would ever know. I crawl out the window after her, gather up the open edge of the bag, twist it tight, and seal it with one of the plastic strips provided for the purpose. It isn't even difficult to drag her across the damp spring grass to the Ag Building's west-side garage door. Which is, as I expected, locked. I leave her there while I go around to the other side and enter, walk through the dark halls, and cross the echo-y shop. By the last bit of daylight coming through the big, dusty windows, I locate the handle on the overhead door, turn it, and roll the door up. She is right where I'd left her, so I drag her in, shut the door, and pull the bag over to the furnace.

I can feel a soft residual warmth radiating from it, and when I open the heavy door, I see that there is a good, thick bed of glowing coals. I shut the door and stand there for a few minutes, thinking.

This is it. This is the last point at which I still have a choice. So far I have been guilty of nothing more than, maybe, a bit of craziness. I can still call somebody, still let things go back to normal. Once I burn the body, I am a criminal. I need to be honest with myself, not cloud the issue with sentimentality or with righteous justifying. I need to stop and think again.

I stand for a few more minutes, taking a long, hard, clear look at the situation. Then I walk to a red-painted cabinet, lift the key from its more-or-less hidden peg, and open the cabinet door. I pick up a can of kerosene from inside. I open the plastic bag, soak Mrs. Decauter's body with the kerosene, and then push her into the furnace. It does take some effort, but I am a strong woman, used to working with my hands and back. I leave the furnace door open and watch it until there's a little whoof of sound from one edge of Mrs. Decauter's designer jacket, and a lick of flame rises, and then I close the door. I stay in the Ag building most of the night, making sure. I feed wood into the fire and push things around until the body is completely consumed. Forensic scientists could probably find bone shards and maybe a film of fat on the inside of that furnace, but they'd have to look for it pretty hard. I am willing to take that chance.

It will be a cinch to do her work and mine; I've been doing it for years. I have her lesson plans to use if I want, and all her tests and quizzes. Not that I'd want to stick to those antiques, but they're there as backup. The worst thing will be covering up for Mrs. Decauter's actual absence, but I believe – I trust – that for the next four weeks, everyone at Gullion High will be so caught up in his or her own quagmire of work, no one will question whether that aggravating old woman who never joined a group or sponsored a club in her eternal (well, not really!) career, is actually in her classroom.

And just think of what I can do, how I can spread around MaryBeth Decauter's money. There are students who need help, and old people in the community… and I think I'll take her last paycheck and buy a monument for DeAnna's grave.

Cousin Linda and the Light-Up Jesus

Linda sits across the picnic table from me and squashes the end of her cigarette in a saucer. Since we don't allow smoking in our house we are on my porch, where it really is a little too cool to sit. It's October 16th, the day after Linda's birthday, and she's come to talk over yesterday's celebration. At least, we were talking about that, but I can see that something is bothering her.

"I swear," she says, jabbing her cigarette against the saucer with a lot of energy. "I can't believe Momma had that nasty thing on her front porch yesterday, right where everybody was bound to see it."

Linda's mother is Aunt Bet, my mother's sister. Mom and Bet have always been as close as sardines in a can, which is partly why Linda and I feel more like sisters than cousins.

Linda's double-wide is set up in Aunt Bet's side yard, so anybody going to Linda's house passes within twenty feet of Aunt Bet's front door. It's a nice house, with pots of red geraniums on her front porch and everything kept as neat as a pin, so I don't know what Linda is upset about.

"What thing?" I ask.

"That thing! That light-up Jesus! I swear, sometimes I think Momma is losing her grip." Linda takes a big sip of iced tea. This is what Linda lives on, cigarettes and iced tea. It keeps her thin, I reckon, but it keeps her nerves jangled too, if you ask me.

"She had that back on her front porch?" I ask. Linda is referring to a life-size plastic figure of Jesus, right hand extended toward the viewer in invitation, left hand poised to tap on whatever surface He's set next to, usually a front door. It is painted in realistic colors and is wired for 110, so you can put a light bulb inside Him and turn Him on at night. Aunt Bet brought it home from a trip to the Smokies last year, that she took with the rest of the senior ladies of the Middle Drive Baptist Church, and it has been a thorn in Linda's flesh ever since.

"I thought she put it away for the fall," I say.

"I put it away for the fall, she drug it out again." Linda's nostrils squeeze together as she takes a deep breath. Then, of course, she has to cough, because she smokes way too many of those cigarettes, they'll be the death of her is what I think, but she takes another sip of tea and says, "The next time I get rid of that thing, it'll stay gone."

I don't want to get in the middle of this, this is Linda's business and her mother's, but I can't help saying, "Well, Linda, it's her porch, and if she wants a plastic Jesus out there, I don't see how it hurts anything."

"It's just silly, is all! That thing drew bugs all summer, we couldn't even set out on the porch in the evenings. And of all things, a plastic Jesus! It's tacky."

Linda knows about decorating. She sold Princess House for years, and started out in Stanley Home Products before that, so she knows whereof she speaks, as they say. Plus, she has a natural ability. I always ask Linda where I should put new pictures on my walls, and get her to help me pick out new wallpaper. I didn't really like it when she painted her kitchen cabinets orange, but other than that one time, Linda's house has always been beautifully decorated. Right now she has her sliding glass doors framed in silk magnolia flowers and greenery, with framed prints of magnolia blossoms flanking. The color of her new couch and love seat is the exact same shade of green as the leaves around the door and in the pictures. She bought coordinating fabric and made throw pillows for each corner of the couch and love seat. The overall effect is really something.

So we drop the subject of Aunt Bet's light-up Jesus and talk about who was at the party and how much weight they've gained, but I can tell Linda's heart isn't in it. The phone rings and I go in to answer it.

"Hello," I say.

"Well, how are you today?" says Aunt Bet. People calling up and starting right in on a conversation without identifying themselves is a favorite complaint of mine, but this is okay, I know this voice instantly.

"Pretty good, I guess. Are you doing okay?"

"Yes, I reckon." Aunt Bet has a heart condition and is supposed to take it easy, but she always overdoes. She keeps her house spotless, and has a big garden every year. She grows enough stuff for her kids to eat out of it too, even though they're all grown and out of the house. She keeps two freezers and a canning room full of food. Nobody can get her to cut back.

"Do you think it'll freeze tonight?" I say.

"Well, it might. I covered my azaleas and set my geraniums back."

We talk some more about the weather, and she asks about Mildred, who is my mom. Then she asks if I have seen Linda today.

"Yes, she's right here," I say.

Aunt Bet chuckles and says, "I thought I might find her up there. Do you think she'd talk to me for a minute?" Aunt Bet has a nice chuckle; it reminds me of the sound of apples poured into a bucket, low-pitched and bumpy.

"I'll just hand the phone to her," I say, and carry the receiver out to the porch.

As I hand the phone to her, Linda whispers, "Who is it?" and I whisper back, "It's your mom." Linda frowns and reaches for the little leather case that holds her cigarettes and lighter. "Hello," she says into the phone, and flips open the flap on the case. She shakes out a cigarette, pulls the lighter out of its special compartment, lights up.

She listens for a few seconds. I can hear Aunt Bet's voice, compacted by the telephone. Then Linda says, "Well, if that's what you want, but I am only going to help you under one condition," like a school teacher talking to a whiny child.

She pauses, says, "Mom, I don't mind helping, but only if you get that Jesus thing off your front porch."

Pause.

"Because," she says, "it's tacky. It makes it look like poor white trash live there."

I sit in the fall sunshine, and pull Tom's old sweater across my chest. I look across my garden, where the turnips are still green but everything else is pretty well gone, to the three flat wooden bears that I have arranged along the driveway. I drew the patterns for those bears on plywood that Tom had left from some project. He cut them out with his jigsaw, and I painted them. I think they're cute, a momma and two cubs, and I have been considering adding an old woman's behind, like she had on big old-fashioned skirts and polka-dot bloomers and was bent over so you couldn't see her head, just her backside. I saw one like that in Janelle Kincaid's yard. Suddenly I am wondering if Linda just might consider four plywood cutouts in one yard tacky. At least my bears don't light up.

"Okay, Mom, I'll be over in a few minutes. Okay. All right. But I mean it about that Jesus. See you later." Linda hands the phone to me. "She wants to speak to you," she says, and drags deep on her cigarette, making the line of glowing orange fire crawl up the white rolled paper.

"Hello?" I say, and Aunt Bet asks if I want to quilt some that afternoon. Aunt Bet and I love to quilt. We use big, old-fashioned quilting frames. I have an extra bedroom and we can put a quilt in the frames and leave it up in there for as long as it takes, whether it's two weeks or all winter. I tell her that would be great, and I stand up to take the phone back in the house, and Linda says she'd better get going, she's got to defrost Aunt Bet's chest freezer. I know Aunt Bet's bad back won't let her bend over long enough to lift out all those bags of frozen squash and peas, or wipe down the sides. Otherwise she wouldn't have asked for help.

"All right," I say. "We're going to quilt this afternoon, you want to come back up and visit while we do it?" This is a formality. Linda doesn't quilt, it's too slow for her, and I know she is not in the mood to visit with her mother.

"No, I've got some things I've got to do. I'll see you later."

"Okay. Call me when you get a chance." This is a formality, too. Aunt Bet's house is not but a good stone's throw from mine, and Linda's is right on the other side of it. We see each other almost every day, and talk on the telephone, too. Linda and I are the closest of all the cousins, despite ten years' difference in our ages. Not that we don't get on each other's nerves sometimes.

Aunt Bet comes up around two o'clock, and we go straight into the bedroom and get started. I thread up eight or ten needles and line them up on Aunt Bet's side of the quilt. She has a hard time getting thread through the little eyes of quilting needles, but she can see well enough to do the stitching. She is the best quilter I know, makes rows of tiny, even stitches, never seems to hurry but covers a quilt quicker than the dew covers Dixie.

We are working on a Lone Star. The star is all shades of gold, set in natural-colored muslin. It is real pretty, if I do say so myself.

Today Aunt Bet is not saying much. The minutes slide by, the square of sunlight coming through the window to lay on the quilt stretches into a long rectangle. I re-thread her needles, we roll up one side of the quilt and then the other. Finally Aunt Bet straightens up and stretches her shoulders. "I guess I'd better get on home," she says, "see what I can find for supper."

"Do you still have some of Linda's birthday cake?" I say. "If you don't, let me give you some. I brought home a big piece, Tom and I shouldn't eat it and the kids won't."

"No, I've still got a piece." She stands up, runs her hands over the area of quilt in front of her. "This is a beautiful quilt. I never thought all those golds would make up so pretty."

"Me too," I say, and we stand and look at it for a few seconds.

"That Linda," Aunt Bet says, tilting her head to look at the quilt from a slightly different angle, "what makes her so hard-headed some times?" Aunt Bet has a very strong policy against speaking ill of others, so I am surprised.

"She gets it from her daddy, I guess." We both snigger. Uncle Ralph had a reputation in his younger days, and Mom and I suspect he gave Aunt Bet a hard row to hoe. Of course, Aunt Bet never let on, but family always knows, or at least suspects.

"She is determined to get rid of my light-up Jesus," she says.

"She doesn't seem to like it much," I venture to say. "Does that shade, that row second from the outside, look too bright to you?"

Aunt Bet walks around to the other side of the quilting frames, tilts her head, squints her eyes. "No, I don't think so. You have to have some bright ones."

I walk to her side, tilt and squint. "Hmm."

"Well, I'll go on. But Linda's going to realize that I can put on my porch what I want to. I'm not that far gone yet."

"You're not so far gone but what you can work rings around me," I say, and give Aunt Bet a one-armed hug. "I believe we can finish this in another day or two."

"Yep, just another day or two," she agrees.

The next day, about mid-morning, I call Linda. The frost came during the night, and I watch out the window as we talk. The leaves are falling off the maples like a bright red snow storm. I tell Linda what I've gotten done this morning, she tells me what she has to do this afternoon. Then she says, "I swear, my mother is driving me crazy."

"She is?" I reply.

"I thought I had the little problem all taken care of." She pauses, I know she's inhaling cigarette smoke. "You know, yesterday I helped her clean out her big freezer."

"Was it messy?" I ask.

"Lord, no! When did my mother ever let a speck of dirt settle in her house? She just decided it needed to be done, you know how she is."

I sort of laugh through my nose, to show I know what she means. Aunt Bet and my mom both keep a clean house. As far as that goes, so do Linda and I.

"So anyway, after we took every last thing out of that freezer, and wiped down the walls with Spic-n-Span, and dried them with a towel, and put everything back in except for one bag of pinto beans that she couldn't remember when she'd put in there, she said she was going up to your house to quilt. I told her that I'd sit on her porch and have a cigarette and then I'd go on home. So she left, and I smoked my cigarette, and then, when she was good and out of sight, I picked up that plastic Jesus and carried Him to my house."

"You did?" I say, surprised. Minding our mommas and treating older people with respect were drummed into both Linda and me at a young and tender age, and this sounded both disobedient and disrespectful.

"Yes, I did." Linda sounds like a bad preacher, full of righteousness. "That thing is ugly, and in the way of her front door. I figured Mom wouldn't even notice that it was gone."

"Did she?"

"I guess so. This morning, I looked out my bathroom window while I was brushing my teeth, before I'd even made up the bed or anything, and there it was, back on her front porch."

"How'd it get there?"

"She must have come and got it and carried it over there. I swear, it's so heavy that I nearly couldn't handle it, and yet she sneaks over here before I'm awake, walks right up on my porch, and hauls it back, without even so much as a Mother-may-I." I hear the sound of Linda blowing smoke, and squashing a cigarette.

"Well, you didn't ask before you took it off her porch," I say in a disinterested tone, like I'm doing something else while I'm talking.

"No, and I won't the next time, either." There's a little click from Linda's side of the connection, the sound of her cigarette lighter being used. "And I'll bet you that the next time I take that thing, it'll stay gone," she adds.

I do not want to add fuel to this fire, so I am very careful as I suggest, "I don't see much harm in letting her have her light-up Jesus. Is it worth getting upset about?"

"Oh, I'm not going to be upset long, I'm going to solve that little problem." Then she changes the subject, so I let it go, and figure that time heals all wounds. This situation will settle out, too.

We hang up and I don't talk to Linda again that day, or the next morning, either. That afternoon I have to go to town to buy groceries and return books to the library and pay the light bill. As I am driving out of town, right where the road turns into four-lane and there's that row of nice brick homes on the right-hand side, I notice there's a big yard sale going on.

I am not a dyed-in-the-wool yard-saler. Some people spend every Saturday going from one to the next, or start in on Fridays, to get to the good stuff before anybody else does. I just go every once in a while.

This day, for some reason, I slow down when I see the sign, then pull in the driveway. I see tables of clothes, some kitchen ware, and a plastic tarp with toys and kids' shoes spread out on it, off to the side. If the lady hadn't been standing right there sorting things, I would have backed out and left, but there she was, watching me, so I push the gear into park and turn off the key. I get out and walk to the nearest table.

"Hello," the lady calls out. "Are you looking for something in particular?"

"No," I say, "I just saw your sign and thought I'd stop for a minute."

"You go right ahead, just yell at me if you need help."

"Okay, thank you," I say, and pretend like I'm interested in some men's sweaters she has laid out there. Tom wouldn't wear a sweater on a bet. Every year or two, somebody gives him a sweater for Christmas, and I put it in a drawer till everybody forgets what it looks like. Then I haul it out and wear it myself. There's a nice green one on the table, with a piece of masking tape with "$1" marked on it stuck to its front, and I wonder if Aunt Bet would like it to garden in. I guess it's because I am thinking about Aunt Bet that causes me not to be surprised when I look across the piles of coats and jackets and see a life-size plastic figure of Jesus.

I pick up the green sweater and walk over to the lady. She is tearing little bits of tape off a roll, sticking them on shirts and pants, and writing prices on them with a stub of pencil.

"Did you find something?" she asks.

"Yes, I'll take this," I say, and lay the sweater down so I can get the money out of my purse. As I'm fishing around for it, I say to her, "That's an interesting figure over there. Is that for sale?"

"What, that plastic Jesus?" she says.

"Uh-huh," I say, stirring up my purse and looking in it like it's a six-feet-deep hole and I'm liable to find buried treasure in it.

"Oh yes, that's for sale, but we hadn't priced it yet. Me and my sister are doing this yard sale together, and she brought that over this morning. I can't figure out where it come from, I've never seen it before. Anyway, she didn't say what she wanted for it. Would you like a bag for that?"

I realize she's referring to the sweater, and I say that would be nice, and as she's putting the sweater into a paper bag from the Food Lion, I stroll over to the Jesus and look Him over. He looks pretty good. I don't see any cracks and His paint's in good shape. He looks the same as Aunt Bet's, one hand extended, the other in mid-knock. There's a cord coming out the bottom of His robe, so I know He's the light-up kind. I turn around and walk back to the lady to pick up the sweater, and I say, very casual, "Well, do you reckon she'd take two dollars for it?"

She pauses, pulls both lips inside her mouth, and looks over at the Jesus. Then her lips pop out and she clicks her tongue and she says, "Yes, I think she would." I don't delay a second, getting the money from my wallet, and as I'm handing the bills over to her, she smiles at me and says, "I guess that'll teach Dorothy to dump her stuff and run off to the store, won't it?"

"I guess so," I say, and I understand her mood exactly.

We load the Jesus into the back of the pickup, and by the time I get home I'm wondering where in the world I can put that thing so nobody will ever know I've got it.

The next morning, Linda calls. "Hel-lo!" she says, "how's every little thing today?"

I tell her that it's too early to tell, yet, and ask what she's been up to.

"Oh, nothing," she says in a tone that means she's been into something delightful.

"Sounds like you've won the Publishers Clearing House," I say.

"On no, nothing like that." Linda blows. She's smoking, of course. "Mom went to prayer meeting last night."

I hadn't thought about it, but Aunt Bet had told me they were having a special prayer circle for Susie Walton, who's got cancer and not expected to live.

"Susie's sister Clevie came by and picked her up, and they went on at about two o'clock. They shopped around and ate supper at Long John's before they went."

"Well," I say.

"Yeah, sometimes it's wonderful to have a little time to myself, I can get so many things done," Linda says.

"Uh-huh," I say. "So what did you get done yesterday, with Aunt Bet gone, that you couldn't have done while she was there?" I am not paying much attention to Linda, I'm trying to get the biscuits in the oven. Holding the biscuit pan, opening the oven door, and holding a telephone receiver between my shoulder and my ear is about stretching my talents to the limit, without keeping up an intelligent conversation.

"Oh, nothing," she says, all light and airy, and she laughs. "Listen," she says, as if I was not, "I'm thinking about asking David's principal over for dinner tomorrow night. Would you let me bring Pumpkin up to your house for a while? He can stay in his carrier, if you'll put him where he can see the TV."

Pumpkin is Linda's cat, a big, fat, orange, neutered male who takes his loss of testosterone out on any strangers who enter what he considers his domain. David is Linda's husband, who went back to school after their kids were born and got a degree and really bettered himself, as he so often points out. He teaches history at the high school, but he would like to get promoted to the assistant principal's job. He'd like to get out of the classroom, he says, kids nowadays are too mean to teach. Inviting Mr. James over for dinner must be a step on the road to the office for David. A yellow-eyed, ankle-biting, shin-clawing, feline sumo wrestler wouldn't help.

So I tell Linda sure, bring old Pumpkin on up. I don't tell her that Tom will be ill as a hornet. He hates that cat like he hates a drought in May. I figure if Pumpkin stays in his carrier, he and Tom can watch the same TV without tearing each other up too bad.

We hang up and I finish fixing breakfast and get Tom out the door to work and the kids off to school. Then, while I am washing dishes, it comes to me what has made Linda so chipper and eager for upper-class company. I go to the living room and pull back the lace inserts that hang behind the front drapes - a window treatment Linda showed me - and look down towards Aunt Bet's. I can't see her porch very well, so I go get the binoculars and come back and look again. Then I sit down at the kitchen counter, with a second cup of coffee, and I think about things.

I usually sit down with a cup of coffee after Tom and the kids are out of the house and I've got the morning work done up. I can't rest with work hanging over me, but once the floors are clean and the beds are made, I can enjoy ten minutes' of relaxation, maybe with a good book or the paper. But I am not reading this morning. I am thinking, and remembering all the hours I've spent at the edge of one quilt or another, talking with Mom and Aunt Bet about everything under the sun, and how Aunt Bet never has a harsh word to say about anybody. I think about all the prayer circles she's been in, and how many casseroles she's taken to sick people's houses, and how she's fed half the county out of her gardens, and never taken one penny in return.

I finish my coffee, and rinse the cup. I put on one of Tom's old sweaters and go out to the garden shed and prop open the doors, then back the pickup up to them. I hoist the light-up Jesus into the bed of the pickup, drive down to Aunt Bet's, and unload the Jesus onto her porch. I take the time to position Him just right, easy to see from the road and close enough to the wall so I can plug in His cord. Then I drive back to our house, park the truck, and go into the shed. There's a good-sized piece of plywood in there, and I drag it into the sun and start sketching out the shape of an old lady's behind, with big, old-fashioned bloomers. Tom can cut this out for me this evening, while Pumpkin's watching TV. I'll bet Tom will know how to rig up a floodlight, too, so my bears and old lady will show up good at night.

The Collector

I am watching the young man in front of me, memorizing him, the way he is at this moment: tall, pushing six feet; slim, with narrow hips and legs, and shoulders that are just beginning to show that they will, with the addition of a few more years and a few more pounds, be solid and strong. Short brown hair, combed away from his face and held in place with some kind of pomade. His eyes – although they are turned away from me I know them well, have already memorized them – are a pretty brown, with flecks of grey and green. His lips, thin; his teeth good but already showing the stains of tobacco smoke.

There is a moment of building. He carefully brings his raised arms, both hands clasped on the grip of a rapier-slim golf club, further back, twisting the thin summer shirt and the muscles at his waist. I imagine I hear creaking, the sound of already twisted ropes being wound a final, vibrating notch. Slowly the end of the club moves another six or eight inches, curving round to almost point towards the boy himself, as if wanting to sneak a peak at him from behind.

He pauses, looks down the range as if his gaze could intimidate the small metal signs that mark off the yards. He shifts his feet and settles them more firmly on the plastic carpet; returns his gaze to the little white ball near his feet; rises onto the toes of his left foot. Pauses, holds this breathless moment of *now*!

I am too young for this; I cannot bear the beauty of it. I want to touch those muscles that pull so sweetly in his back beneath the cotton shirt, to bring his intensity to bear on me. I step forward, reach out, draw breath to speak, to say something that will return him to me – he's so intent on what he's doing he's gone away from me – remind him that I am here and am important too.

Before I reach him, he swings.

It is so swift I do not even see the club's motion. I had not anticipated the power of the swing, or understood the concentrated force. I had forgotten, even, that the point here is for the boy to pour his energy into a hit. "I can hit the ball as hard as I can, and no one tells me not to," he'd once said.

The lump of metal and wood, moving too fast for sight, breathes into my hair as it passes. It slides down my cheek tenderly, a lover's touch that my uterus recognizes and responds to, before my mind even understands what has happened. I am shocked into still-ness. Unable to scream, cry, fall, breathe, I stand.

And then, I wake up.

My forty-year-old heart is thumping as hard as it did that night when I was sixteen, and I wonder if this is the time the dream sets off a real heart attack, the one I've been expecting for years. At least since Aunt Jean died at age 36, and then Aunt Min at 32. My mother is healthy at 65, but still I feel the cardiac cards are stacked against me.

"What?" my husband says. His eyes are still closed, his voice rough with sleep.

"Nothing," I whisper. "Just a dream."

He doesn't even turn over, slides back into deep sleep. I lift the covers carefully, slip out of bed, go to the computer in the dining room and turn it on. I have three new e-mails.

"Mrs. Monroe," the first begins, "a friend forwarded your website address to me and suggested I contact you. Last year when I was in the hospital I had what I think is called an out-of-body experience, when my spirit left my body and floated over the heads of the people who were in the room with me. I could see and hear them all quite clearly, and have a perfect recollection of what was said and done at that time, though I was technically (medically) unconscious."

I need to work on my website. I keep getting these contacts from people who have "died" and come back, and they all want to tell me what it's like "on the other side." I know their families have gotten tired of hearing about it. How many times can you hear about someone's transfiguration before it begins to sound like mere fear? Repetition can wear a thing out, whether it's a pair of shoes or the recitation of a miracle.

At my site and in newspaper ads and, a few times, in person at small gatherings, I ask people who have experienced another kind of event to contact me. I'm not interested in religious revelations or conversations with Jesus or even in how uplifting death will be. I realize those subjects deserve the attention of a researcher or a psychologist or even – I can't imagine why this hasn't been done – a serious religious investigator, but that is not my aim. I am seeking people who have come close to death but not died. I am not interested in the afterlife, but in the now-life. Since I was sixteen and in love with the boy from up the road, I have known that an event like that should – must – mark its victim.

One should be able to recognize them, these extraordinary people. They become different, armed with a special weapon against the forces of the mundane. They are not like the rest, the poor unchosen, or are like them but with something extra, something wonderful and fey. It is something that I either missed or failed to accept as it was proffered, or have but do not realize. Though it would seem I meet the one requirement, something prevents my membership in the corps of the elite, this hidden-in-plain-sight tribe.

After years of seeking this difference in myself, I realized I might learn to recognize it by finding it first in others. Other people, surely, had missed death by the thinnest of chances. There must be people who would have died if they'd stepped one step closer to the highway's edge, would have fallen into a suddenly gaping pit if they'd not stopped to admire a rainbow, would have died of snakebite if they'd reached for the Easter egg hidden under *that* leaf instead of *that* one. Surely, if I found some of these people and talked to them, studied them, I could discover what it is that makes them special and then see it in myself.

I ran that ad in the classified listings of six newspapers in a hundred-mile radius. The number of people who responded was disappointing but not surprising. How can the elite be elite if there are many of them? And most of those who responded were weirdos. There's no other word for them, collectively. Some wanted to convert me to their religions, some wanted to sell me their versions of incidents they'd probably made up. A few would have sold me anything. How many drug addicts are living around here, anyway? And it's shocking how many people believe they have been in contact with aliens from other planets, dimensions, galaxies. A very few had done as I had done, coming so close to Death as to smell his breath, but then been excused:

"I was driving north on I-81 one day, and I moved into the left lane to pass a dark blue Honda. I pulled ahead of him, signaled before I got back into the right-hand lane. As I checked my rearview mirror to make sure I was far enough ahead of the Honda to return to that lane, I saw the front hood of the Honda flip up. As I watched, it came loose, slammed into the Honda's windshield and then rolled up onto the car's roof and sailed off the back edge. It crashed into the car that was just behind the Honda. The driver of the Honda lost control; his car went careening into the median and the south-bound lanes, where it was crushed by a tractor-trailer. Other cars piled into the wreckage. The second car, the one that had been behind the Honda, skewed off in the opposite direction, onto the shoulder, bounced off the guardrail and back into the north-bound lanes, spun around and was hit head-on by at least one car.

"If I had waited three seconds more to pass the Honda, I would have been behind it when its hood came off. I would have died."

That one was what I was looking for. And another:

"When I was a kid, my cousin and I were fooling around at a construction site. Everyone wanted to see where the new mall was going to be built; it was an irresistible attractor for everyone, young, old. Whatever. It was near my cousin's house, and we had gone there alone because the older kids had run away from us. My cousin was telling me where to walk, how to stay safe, and was trying to scare me too, which was what her brothers and sister had done to her. So it was all, 'If you get too close to the edge of that ditch you'll fall in and the bulldozers will cover you up and you'll die, buried alive in the ditch,' and 'if you step in that mud it'll give way under you, and there's no bottom to it, ever, you'll just sink and sink until you die but they'll never find your body,' and 'you see those red wires on the ground there? Well, those are the wires that connect the dynamite to the firing pin, and if you step on one of those red wires, there'll be a big explosion and you'll be gone, smashed to smithereens.' And although I told myself not to believe her because she was a liar, the possibility of danger made being there more fun and exciting and besides, what if she was right, this one time? We were walking along, she was a little bit ahead, and suddenly she turned around and her face went weird and she screamed, 'Stop! Stop, don't step there!' And I looked down, and my foot was right above one of the red wires…"

My husband and I have argued about this. I didn't tell him about my experience before we married, or about my deep interest in its effects. It is, as I am sure you understand, difficult to explain. We'd been married for three years and he was confident in his right to know everything about me, every aspect of my personhood, when he asked what I so often was writing about.

I told him it was nothing. That it was nothing that he'd be interested in. That it was private. That if I felt it was anything he should know or, for that matter, that was his right to know, I would have shared it with him earlier. Then he demanded to know how long I'd been working on this secret project, and although at first I resisted telling him even that, I finally said it had been a few years. Yes, since before we were married. No, no one else knew. No, I did not want to talk to him about it.

In the end, I did, a little. Months dragged by, and he was continually letting his feelings be hurt by my separate and secret interest. To his credit, he never accused me of having an affair, but it was as if keeping any of myself discrete from the life he and I shared, equaled some kind of betrayal. Whatever piece of me that wasn't open to his perusal, was part of me that must be participant in something actively anti-us. So he said.

Eventually, I tried – but failed - to explain. At least he mostly stopped asking me about it. He even offered up his own incident:

"I was just a kid, eight or ten years old. My dad and I had gone fishing, up on Foster Creek. We were above the falls there, and about ten feet from the drop-off. There were these big rocks that were in a kind of row across the stream. So I held my rod and reel in one hand and hopped across to the far side of the stream and fished for a little while, and then I decided to cross back over. And about half way across, my right foot just slid off that rock and I nearly went down into the water. Man, I was scared! I could have gone right over that waterfall, a drop that was every bit of 40 feet. Thirty-five, anyway."

I thanked him for the information and stood up to go to the kitchen, to finish clearing away after supper. He followed me and after watching me put all the dishes from the dishwasher into the cabinets, asked if I was going to write his story down in my notebook. No, I said, hoping he'd let it go. Why not? he asked, and then I had to try to explain without hurting his feeings. It wasn't the same. He wouldn't have died, probably; he father was right there, the stream too shallow, the fall too short. He hadn't been scared.

"I was scared!"

Not enough.

"What do you mean? I was a kid and I was scared shitless, that's what. What would make it enough?"

Did it change your life?

He turned away, and after that, he didn't ask about my work very much.

"Haimish and I were out riding the four-wheeler. We were going up this hill. It wasn't all that steep and we weren't going very fast. And then suddenly, it flipped. The front end just rose up into the air and Ham and I were on the ground and I was thinking, this thing is going to fall right down on me and kill me or I'm going to be paralyzed for the rest of my life or something. It was just coming right over on top of us, like it was in slow motion. And then I thought that if I could just push on the back of the driver's seat – it was right over me – and if I could just use my feet and legs to push that sucker up and over, it might go past me. I even had time to wonder if Ham was behind me, because if he was and I was successful in getting that vehicle to land somewhere beyond me, it might land on him. And I thought, 'Fuck it, Ham can look after himself.' I did the thing with my feet and sure enough, the four-wheeler landed behind me. I never got a scratch. Haimish didn't either – he was lying off to my left, somewhere. It was just so weird. It was like everything stopped, like I was outside of time or something. And who would've come up with the idea of trying to move a four-wheeler with his feet and legs like that? I can't get it out of my mind, either."

Yes, I want to say. I know, I know. It's there, just outside your peripheral vision, just waiting. Waiting so you can take it into the front of your mind and give it attention. So you can find the point of entry and tap it or push it or whatever it is that is required, and understand.

The first few times, I'd simply asked if they felt their experiences had made them different. Of course, the question was too broad, and I got every kind of answer, from an exasperated look to a lecture on God's plans for each of us.

In fact, I get that answer a lot. I've begun –reluctantly – to accept the possibility that they may be right, that God (I haven't started to consider exactly what that word may mean) has a script written for every person, but if so, then are near-death experiences parts of these plans, or is it that the plans are nearly changed by…what? Chance? Satan? Either way, what are we to learn from these situations? And is it something that is imparted to us, intact and whole, if only we'll open the package? Or is it something that we can only have if we work to discover and understand it, and maybe we'll get part – a glimmer, or half, or almost all - of it?

God, if you're out there, what am I supposed to do with this thing?

A man came today. He knocked on the frame around my front door and when I came downstairs I could see his shape but not his face through the screen: he was big, wearing some kind of light jacket. I didn't open the door as I said "Hello? Can I help you?"

He paused a moment, almost too brief a pause to notice, then said, "Are you the one who's collecting people's stories?" His voice was accentless, low but clearly audible.

I did not open the door. "Yes," I said. Waited. I could see his outline clearly, but his face was backlit and indiscernible.

Another pause, this one a bit more obvious than the first. As if he wanted me to be sure, this time. Then, "I have one."

"One?"

He leaned back a little, which let the light reflect on his face. Pleasant but not striking. His jacket was denim, a light blue shirt underneath, moderately-worn jeans below. Some kind of boots. Clothing that thousands of men wear, feel comfortable in. A kind of uniform, really. "A narrow escape from death," he said.

Something made me wait, although I was interested. This person carried himself with an air, an aura, and deep down I wondered if this would be the one who could show me what I have missed. I have spent so many years living at a remove from life as I know it should be. I have been shortchanged by pale, ordinary life when I know I was selected to have more. I have yearned for the difference and struggled to find it in every person I've met, in every place I've visited, in every situation I've observed. I've hunted carefully for it, sought out those people whom I know must have been cast into that light by a brush-up with ending. But in every case I've been disappointed. Education, marriage, a child, none of it has brought me to the light that I yearn for, that I now wonder – that I suspect – this man has. Finally, after all this time, the years and disillusionment, would he tell me? How to find that air and carry it with me, so that at their lowest level, the level of the gut and its instincts, people will recognize me? So I can recognize myself.

Has the time now come for me? Is he the one?

"When did the incident occur?" I ask. I intend the question to be cool, my voice to be distant, but my stirring interest betrays me.

"Last year," he says, and he does not hesitate at all. "I was working construction, on a high-rise up in Baltimore."

"Just a minute," I say, and I take three steps to the hall table and pick up a notebook and pen. I go to the door, open it, step out onto the porch. I move to the green plastic chairs and sit down in one. Open the notebook, look up at him. "Do you mind working out here?" I say.

"I don't mind."

"Why don't you sit down?"

He sits in the other chair. He seems a little uncomfortable doing it, like he doesn't think it will hold him up.

"What is your name?" I ask. The pen is ready to record.

He looks past me. "I was working on the second floor, using red brick to lay up a fireplace façade."

I see now that his eyes are dark. Brown, or maybe black, I cannot tell pupil from iris.

"Red brick are years out of style. I don't know why the builder chose them."

He glances at me, then quickly away.

"Two floors is as far as the assistants can toss up the bricks. They throw them up, one at a time. The masons catch them, line them up, use a grabber to carry eight or ten at a time over to where we're working. We pulley up loads of mud." Another quick glance. I am not taking notes; I am listening. "Mortar. By the end of the day, the assistants are tired and their tosses are going wild.

"The funny thing is, catching brick is my favorite part of working up high. If everybody does it right, there's a rhythm and it's like the bricks just fall into our hands, like it's their destiny to land right there, soft as rain, right into our hands.

"But late in the day, everybody's tired. The timing is off. That day, I missed one, and was leaning over to pick it up. The assistant threw the next one, and it hit me square in the forehead. I saw it coming. Had time to think, 'Oh, that's going to hit me.' Then it did, and what I remember feeling was not pain, but a hard push."

The man raises his right hand, draws it back nearly to his shoulder, holds it with the fingers slightly curled and the palm facing out: an old television Indian preparing to say "How." Then he slams his hand forward until it meets some invisible surface and he says, softly, "Pow." His heads falls back, propelled by his palm that hit the air two feet away from his face. Or by memory.

Heartbeats of time pass, and then I lean forward. "How?" I ask, and I am tempted, for one split second, to hold up my hand, palm outward. I could almost giggle. "How did you feel afterwards?"

The man looks at the porch floor, or his boots, or at the spider scuttling towards the screen door. "I didn't feel anything for a while. I fell off the building, two floors down. Woke up in the hospital. Doctors said it was a miracle, all that." His tone tells me this part is unimportant. I hope he's not going to say he floated above his body, saw it all happening. "While I was out, unconscious, something happened."

I lean back. Another one, I think. I am so disappointed.

"I heard a voice."

The doctors, the sobbing wife, the child who asks his father to return. I've heard of them before.

"It was cold. I remember being so cold, wishing somebody would turn the heat up, or give me a blanket. I wanted one of my grandmother's quilts."

I lay the pen down, quietly.

"Then somebody said, 'Tag. You're it.'"

What? "What?"

He closes his eyes now. "Everything's been different, ever since," he says. "I am different."

I have sensed this, almost from the first. He is different. He has what I have been so longing to have. I wait.

"I am Death," he says. "I'm here to collect." He leans forward and kisses me full on the lips.

I am watching the young man in front of me, memorizing him: slim, with narrow hips and legs, short brown hair combed away from his face. He carefully raises his club, looks down the range, swings.

I do not even see the club's motion, it is so swift. Unable to scream, cry, breathe, I fall.

Plowing with Horses

light – n. that form of radiant energy that stimulates the organs of sight.

One day when I was 46 years old, my mother turned one bright brown eye – that so neatly matched my two –towards me and said, "I used to plow with horses."

She was 71 years old at that time, and her eye was so very bright because she'd just had a cataract removed from it. All the way home from the hospital, with me behind the wheel of her little blue Honda car, she'd been reading the road signs to me.

"Howard Johnsons, 36 flavors of ice cream!"

She said she had not realized how dark her world had become. She could see the signs!

"Abingdon, five!"

"Virginia Highlands Community College, next exit!"

And then that line about plowing. I glanced to the right and to the left of the highway, to see what she was reading, but there was nothing but a pasture with black beef cattle fattening in it, and far off on top of the ridge that rolled parallel to the interstate, a little man on a toy tractor, pulling brown dirt up from the green field behind it.

"You plowed with horses?" I asked. She'd never mentioned this before.

I remembered my grandfather well, and the two Ford tractors he'd owned in succession, with which he'd accomplished all the heavy work on the 70 acres that my mother had inherited.

"I hated those horses. Sam and Bill, and Bill was as mean as a snake. He'd puff up so I couldn't get the harness cinched tight, and then he'd tangle his feet in the lines. He did it on purpose. And sometimes he'd kick."

"You never told me you used horses on the farm. Or that you had to do the plowing." Mom had talked to me plenty of times about her young life. It was pretty dramatic, with a mother who died young and the Depression and all that. She'd never said a thing about working horses.

"Daddy always wanted sons to help him do the work, and carry on with the farm after he was gone," she intoned, "but he only had daughters."

I'd heard that before, and had decided long ago that my grandfather had been pretty short-sighted. Had he not known it was perfectly legal to leave his land to a daughter? Did he think he couldn't hire some help, if he needed it? As it turned out, he divided the farm up and left it to the girls anyway, even if he did live long enough that all four of them already owned places of their own and didn't need his farm after all. And they'd all married men who had pitched in to help with the hay and tobacco on Grandpa's farm as necessary.

Then Mom added something else I had not heard before. "He didn't want us to get married, but Doris married Darrell just to get away from home. Then Susie ran off with the Colonel. Your daddy was courting me and Grandpa told me that if I wouldn't get married, he'd buy a new tractor and teach me to drive it, and I wouldn't have to plow with the horses any more."

"And how'd it turn out?" I asked, even though the answer was obvious. I mean, there I was, driving her up the interstate, undeniable evidence that my mother had indeed married my father. Or at least had had a serious relationship with him.

"Well, I didn't tell him that I would or I wouldn't. Daddy went ahead and bought the tractor, and then I married your father."

"I guess Grandpa was disappointed," I said. I might've sounded the least bit smug. Grandpa, adored as he was by his daughters, was always distant and cold to me. I had always had to sit quietly in his presence, and had had to help chop thistles out of his pasture fields.

"Well, he had probably already decided to buy a tractor anyway," Momma said, looking straight ahead, with her one good eye and her one clouded one. The doctors had said it would be better to fix them separately, so she would only have one eye bandaged up at a time, and could see to get around. "Lord, I hated those horses."

light – n. enlightenment. Mental or spiritual illumination.

I stood at the edge of the plowed part of the field, waiting for Mr. Richardson and his team to make the turn and head back in my direction. That would be a good shot, with the long faces of the horses, their eyes cupped by blinders, leading the way, the man's shoulders and cap-covered head behind.

The team and their driver turned, trod steadily back across the sloping field, made the near turn and headed back toward the far edge. I let my camera hang on its cord around my neck, and tilted my face to the sun. Sometimes I loved this job. When it meant getting out of the office and away from the courthouse and sheriff's office, getting a sweet little story that I knew people in the county would enjoy reading, when it all came together like this... What's not to love? I asked myself. I kept my eyes closed and concentrated on the smells. Good damp dirt, fresh-turned; spring grass bruised by hooves and boots; clean air from over the little creek, carried by its own weight to the bottom of the hill; and the combined odors of the healthy, working horses and the leather harness that connected them with the plow and the man.

I had enjoyed talking to Steve Richardson. At 61, he seemed not older than his years, but older than his time. He and his little clapboard house, and his immaculate garden, and even his well-greased workboots and bibbed overalls, wouldn't have been out of place if they'd been time-jumped backwards forty years, or eighty years.

His horses were Morgan - Belgian crosses. They were not the giants of beer commercials or Renaissance fairs, but were plenty big enough to pull a plow for an afternoon, or to get to the barn with a wagon-load of burley tobacco strung on sticks. They were neat, and seemed just the right size for hillside fields and one-man farms. As a result of his steady training, they were calm and willing to work. I'd watched him harness them, seen how they moved into position almost without his direction. I had sensed that these horses knew their work and found some deep pleasure in it. I'd jotted down a few lines about them as I'd watched them heading for the field, about how they knew their importance in the scheme of this farm, and about how Steve Richardson didn't spoil them or fuss over them like pets, but took care of them with respect and worked in tandem with them.

I opened my eyes and watched how the animals powered the plow together. Steve had told me that horses don't pull a plow, but push it, and now I could see what he'd meant. The big leather collars distributed the resistance of the plow sliding into the earth onto the horses' shoulders as they leaned into them. When the horses turned and headed away from me, I saw the broad hips squat; huge muscles bunched and rolled, and the plow slid forward. The horses pushed against the neck collars, not pulled the plow behind them. It was a much more efficient use of energy.

At the next near turn, Steve stopped the horses and came over to me.

"You want to try it?" he asked.

"Me? Plow?"

"Yeah."

"I don't know how." I really wanted to do this, but.

"Aw, give it a try. It's the only way to learn."

"Well. What if I mess things up?" Please make me do this, I thought.

"Go on, now."

I walked up slowly and picked up the lead lines. The horses' heads came up and I thought, oh shit.

"Pull 'em up a little tighter. Just don't let the lines get down around their hooves, or under the plow."

I slid my hands further up the warm leather straps and was just beginning to wonder whether I should say 'Giddyup' or shake the lines or something, when from where he was standing at the edge of the field, Steve Richardson said in a calm, not-very-loud voice,

"Come ahead, boys," and the horses started.

I had to step quickly to keep up. (Steve hadn't looked like he was hurrying. I was feeling like I was always half a step behind.) I wondered wildly if I should pull on one lead line or the other, to keep the horses headed straight. I had a moment of panic when I realized I would have to turn the horses when we came to the end of the furrow.

I actually did neither. From his position thirty or forty feet away, Steve called commands to the horses and they obeyed him. I think they would have made the right moves, even if Steve had not spoken them aloud; his calls were probably more for my comfort than for the horses' guidance.

They made the furrow, they turned, they came back, and when we reached the end of the row and Steve called, "Come up, boys," they stopped. I was panting; they were not. I had kept the lines out from under their feet, and I had stepped lively, and I had hung on. They had done all the real work. I was shaky and sweating, but it was from excitement.

Because what I had felt running through those leather lead lines was power.

The horses were not huge, but were concentrated. They were strength – a lot of strength – contained, shaped and formed so that no space was wasted; everything in them was streamlined and devoted almost exclusively to the purpose of work.

And all of that, all of that strength and potential and calm intelligence and shared intent, had for those few minutes been delivered down the leather lines to my hands and it had caused my heart to race and my skin to ripple like pond water. Power.

light – n. something with which to enkindle

We argued about a motorcycle for nearly twelve years. During that time I went through stages of hating motorcycles and nearly hating him; of being so mad at him that I took a tae kwan doh class to try to get rid of some of it; of lying awake at night planning his funeral after the wreck that I knew was inevitable; and of realistically figuring out how I could pay the mortgage after a divorce. And yet in the end, despite my best efforts and my genuine, reasonable issues, he bought a motorcycle and signed up to go on a five-day, 600-mile trip with his buddies.

I hadn't even realized he had buddies. In fact, he probably didn't have buddies until he got that motorcycle: some kind of package deal that nobody warned me about. I didn't expect him to enjoy that trip, either. He never had been a man to spend a lot of time with other men, unless they were working together. But off they'd gone, and despite getting rained on and having to admit that having the smallest bike (by about 500 cc's) meant he could barely keep up on the interstates, my husband of 30 years fell in love with road tripping on a motorcycle. I, of course, still worried about wrecks and bodies that are forced to slide across pavement and what happens when motorcycles tangle with tractor-trailer rigs at 70 miles per hour, but I'd had my say before he got the bike. After that, I kept quiet and made sure the insurance was up to date.

One day he offered to take me for a ride.

I thought about it. I was tempted, not because I'd ever had the itch to ride one, but because... Well, because I thought my coolness factor would go up if I tried it once, and I wanted to be part of the buddy thing, and because... To be real honest about it, because I was jealous of those guys getting such a chunk of my husband's free time. So I went.

First of all, riding behind someone on a motorcycle is sexy. You sit with your breasts pressed against his body, your legs squeezing his, and your crotch on top of a warm, vibrating leather seat. Don't let anybody tell you otherwise. And if it happens that you already have a long history of good sex and genuine love for that person in front of you? Well.

Secondly, not only might your own coolness factor go up, but the guy driving, even if he's a retiree and a little soft in the love handles, will seem hotter for being astride that thing.

The third thing is power. It took about twenty minutes into the ride for me to make the connection. It had been eight or ten years since I'd written the article about Steve Richardson and his team of neat little horses, and felt the power of their bodies communicating down the leather lines to my hands. And here it was again, less elegant maybe, but more visceral; hot, throbbing, without the focus of necessity or usefulness and with more of the wildness of freedom.

I knew I'd never try to talk him out of riding again. I hadn't changed my mind about how dangerous it was. I would worry about him every second that he was on that bike. If I'd been willing to admit my deep-seated superstitious beliefs, I might even say... but I won't even let it form in my mind. But I'll never ask him to not.

It has to do with growing up, and with my mother being given the choice of either horses or a tractor but not of escape, and with how strength can not be created out of thin air but can sometimes be fed by a spark.

Betty and the Chicken Come Home

When Betty Louise Reeves moved back to Highlands County after living in the greater metropolitan area of Baltimore for thirty-five years, there were two things she refused to leave behind. One was her 1991 Lincoln Towncar, even though she figured it would stand out like a sore thumb among all the mud-spattered pickups and compact cars belonging to the cousins back home, and the other was her gynecologist. She was not about to let some strange man get interested in her private parts at this stage of her life, doctor or civilian, so once a year she made the trip to Baltimore, to Doctor Kahn's office, and had her Pap smear and mammogram, and nobody back home got a peek or a hint.

That's how she happened to be driving north on I-95, halfway between the Capital Beltway and the Baltimore Beltway, at 9:46 AM on Monday, November 16. She was on her way to her annual appointment and somehow she got stuck behind a tractor-trailer rig full of chickens. The chickens were jammed together in cages stacked four or five high, and little white feathers were continually blasted off the ill-fated birds onto Betty's windshield, where they slid up the tinted glass like dry, elongated snowflakes.

"Drat," Betty said as she checked for the umpteenth time to see if she could safely pull into the left-hand lane and get around the truck. There was a solid line of traffic as far as she could see in the little convex mirror, and the green Volvo station wagon that had kept her penned in for fifteen minutes was still six feet away from the Towncar's back door handle.

She was fed up with the feathers and the traffic and the truck fumes, which she could smell even inside her Lincoln with the air conditioning going, when suddenly she heard and felt a heavy thump and there, instead of little whisky feathers on her windshield, was an entire chicken body. It lay pressed against the slanted glass on the passenger side for only a few seconds before it flipped off into the grill of the Volvo. Betty kept the Lincoln firmly under control while flicking her eyes to the side mirror to see what would happen next, and she felt a momentary tingle of satisfaction as the bird hit and the driver of the Volvo nearly lost control in the nova of white feathers.

Betty would have known to expect that blast of feathers. She had been born and raised in the country, after all, and in her day had seen more than one chicken run over. They always exploded like that, just went into fifty million pieces. There was nothing for a driver to do then but keep going. The worst thing was, if there was anything much of a carcass left in the road, all the other chickens would come running to check it out, and before you knew it another car would come along and another old hen would meet her Maker in a burst of glory.

But even Betty was taken aback when another bird landed on her windshield. It thudded against the glass with one round golden eye precisely in line with Betty's own. The chicken lay spreadeagled slightly above the speedometer, mere inches from Betty's hands on the steering wheel, and glared at Betty for a full fifteen seconds before it blinked and tried to lift its head.

Betty's hands flew off the steering wheel, but driving skills honed by years of taking three sons to football practice in urban Baltimore were still in place, so she grabbed it back immediately. The heavy Lincoln stayed straight and true, but Betty couldn't see a thing but bird, so she hit the brakes, realized instantly that was a mistake, stepped on the gas, heard a horn blast from the car behind her, and involuntarily let her hands wobble slightly on the wheel. The car obediently followed her guidance, and swayed from side to side in her lane. The car behind Betty honked again and yet again, while the chicken tried to dig its claws into the windshield as it slid six inches to the left, then six inches to the right.

Now nearly panicked, Betty smacked the little button that turned on her hazard lights, then pressed the turn signal lever to indicate a right turn and began to gradually slow. She pulled onto the shoulder of the road, barely missing a hunk of retread rubber that lay like a barricade between Betty and the shoulder's out-of-traffic safety, and finally stopped the car. The chicken slid down the windshield and lay with its feet clutching the wiper blade, wings outstretched, beak open, gasping.

Betty was breathing hard, too.

She took a few minutes to collect herself, then glanced in the mirror to check on her hair, which was still in good shape. She took a deep breath and held it for a second, to help slow down her heart. Betty thought that if that little blonde nurse in Doctor Kahn's office took her blood pressure right then, they'd have her on medication so fast it'd make her head spin. But she was all right. Thank God she hadn't wrecked, and thank goodness she always left plenty of time to get to her appointments. You never know when an emergency will come up.

She looked at the cause of her near escape. The chicken was still on her windshield, still breathing hard, but holding up its head and looking around, even if in a slightly dazed manner. The bird's hairdo hadn't held up as well as Betty's. The feathers were all ruffled and there were obvious gaps where feathers had been blown away and pale, pimply skin showed. The bird's chest was heaving.

"Bet your blood pressure's a little elevated right now, too," Betty said out loud. She took a deep breath, blew out hard, and muttered, "Lord." After another minute Betty brushed her shoulders and chest for stray hairs and potential lint, put the Lincoln in drive, and said, "Okay, chicken, the free ride's over. I've got places to go, so take off."

The chicken had its beak shut now, and was looking at the world over first one shoulder and then the other. Its wings were still sprawled, its feet clenched around the wiper.

"Go on! Shoo!" Betty flapped her hands near its head, but the chicken was looking the other way and didn't notice.

"Chicken!" Betty yelled, but the bird didn't seem to hear. "Hey you! Move it!"

Betty frowned and pushed on the car's horn. A short burst of sound erupted from under the hood, but the chicken merely squatted lower over her clenched feet. Betty let the car roll forward a few feet, but this produced no reaction from the hen at all.

Betty thought for a moment, stepped sharply on the gas and immediately on the brake. The car leaped forward and then slammed to a stop. The chicken swayed and squawked, but hung on.

"Drat," Betty whispered. She pushed the gear stick into park, unclasped her seat belt, and got out of the car. She walked around the door and stood looking at the bird on her windshield.

Up close, the chicken looked bad. It was bedraggled, and obviously befuddled. It didn't seem to know what to do, and didn't move its wings even when Betty wrapped a Kleenex around her index finger and pushed at the bird.

"I'll bet you've been raised in a cage so tight you don't even know what wings are for. Maybe you've never even walked around." Betty studied the sorry piece of under-muscled aviation. "Here," she said, "you've been given a new lease on life. Get off there and make a go of it."

Betty looked for a stick to push the bird off her car, and as she did she noticed for the first time where she was. For miles around the highway lay a grid of access roads and roads that crossed or met the access roads, pimpled by dozens of the kinds of businesses that required big parking lots and big tin buildings: roofing contractors, auto paint shops, second-rate building supply stores, and places that had tires stacked and piled and heaped and strewn about. As far as Betty could see, the biggest piece of actual dirt with plants growing on it was the strip between the north and south lanes of I-95. Even there, there wasn't enough plant life to leave behind a weed stalk big enough for Betty to use to lever the chicken off her windshield.

"Well, it may not be chicken heaven, but it's what you got," she said to the bird. "It's no worse than the processing plant you were headed to, I guess." She studied the chicken for another moment, then leaned into the car and opened the glove box. She took out two large, heavy napkins from Burger King, folded them over her hands, reached out and picked up the bird. She remembered how to do that, from her days on the farm. She knew to hold the wings against the bird's body, and to support it under the breast.

Betty held the bird, which weighed considerably less than she'd expected, away from her good suit. "Live long, and prosper," she said, and tossed the bird toward the embankment.

Any normal bird would have instinctively opened its wings and flown away. Betty didn't expect a chicken to sail off into the blue with grace and a heartfelt expression of gratitude, but she didn't expect it to fall like a dropped potato, either. Which is what it did. Never flapped its wings, not even a flutter. There was a small thud and a brief rattling of coarse dried grass when it hit the ground.

"Drat." Betty squeezed the napkins into each other and stood looking at the place where the chicken had dropped. She wiped her palms with the wadded napkins. She wouldn't have killed it if she could have helped it. She hadn't thought it would just fall like that. Stupid thing. A city chicken, through and through, didn't even know enough to spread its wings to save itself. Probably wouldn't have lived anyway, after taking a beating in the back of that truck for who knew how long. It must be dead now, after such a fall coming on top of the ride in the truck, not to mention the flight to her windshield.

Still, Betty gazed at the place where the bird had fallen, and there, after a few seconds, appeared the bird's head, its vestigial comb and wattles dusty and faded, its eyes blinking.

Betty watched as the bird's head wobbled above a tuft of grass. Then she opened the back door of her Lincoln, smoothed the wadded napkins, and spread them on the floor in front of the back seat. She walked to the tattered chicken, picked it up in her bare hands, and carried it back to the Lincoln. She laid it gently on the spread napkins, shut the back door, and got back in the driver's seat. As she pulled into the north-bound traffic, she spoke sternly to the bird. "Well, I guess I can at least bury you in some good dirt in Highlands County."

When Betty returned to the Lincoln after her check-up, she glanced in the back floorboard and was surprised to see the little white chicken sitting up. Betty always came out of these appointments in a bad mood. Often, the slightest thing would make her cry, and Betty would get mad at herself for such silliness. Today the sight of that slim, tattered bird, its beak open and its skimpy chest heaving, made her eyes fill. Betty crossed her arms and supported her own ample breasts, and remembered how the doctor had pressed and shoved them around in his detached way. She sniffed and blinked and told herself to get a grip on more than just the car door handle. She opened the front door and was hit in the face with the realization that it had gotten hot inside the closed car. She stood for a full minute, looking at the bird and frowning, then shut the car door and marched back into the medical building. She quickly re-emerged, carrying a small paper cup.

She unlocked and opened the back door and set the cup on the napkins in front of the bird. It didn't act scared, didn't flap or squawk. It eyed the cup in what seemed to Betty to be a fierce manner, its head turned so its left eye was aimed straight at the cup. It turned to check the cup with its right eye, then slowly extended its neck - which exposed more of its ugly, bare skin - then suddenly jabbed its head into the cup. It sat back and calmly smacked its beak.

"Tastes pretty good, doesn't it?" Betty said. "For city water, I mean."

The bird stabbed into the cup again, swallowed, shook a drop of water off its beak while gazing into the distance. Betty was reminded of certain of her Baltimore friends who always had to check out the surroundings while they sipped Pepsi through a straw. The bird drank again, and again, then began to straighten the feathers on its chest.

"Maybe that's what I need, too," Betty muttered as she reached in the retrieve the cup. When she was buckling the seat belt across her lap, she added, "Tell you what, if you'll stay alive till we get back home, I'll turn you loose in the country. Shoot, I might even buy you some laying mash. Chicken manna. What do you think?" Without waiting for an answer, Betty let the Lincoln glide onto the street, and pointed its nose toward home.

The chicken held on, and although it wouldn't touch the crumbs from the bun of Betty's Whopper, it continued to drink water. They pulled into the asphalt driveway of Betty's new doublewide late that night, and Betty found a cardboard box that she lined with newspapers. She set the box just inside her back door and carried the bird in, laid it gently in the box, and went to bed. She was exhausted, and half convinced the bird would be dead by morning. She told herself she didn't care. She'd done her part by getting the bird to Highlands County, where it would at least see sky and feel grass beneath its scrawny yellow claws - or grass could grow over its sorry white carcass, if it died during the night.

But the next morning, when Betty passed by the box on her way to make coffee, the bird was sitting up. Betty leaned over and stared at it, and the bird looked right and left, then cocked her head up and glared at Betty. "Well. There you are," Betty said, and the bird shook its head wildly, as though trying to dislodge a parasite from its remaining plumage.

"Don't shake your head at me, you old biddy," Betty returned. "You fool with me, I'll give you to Roosevelt Blevins, and he'd have you plucked and in the pot so fast you'd never know what hit you." The bird ignored this comment, and raised itself slightly on its legs, made a small wet deposit on the newspapers, then scooted forward just enough to clear the mess and sat down again. It began to groom its wing feathers.

"Same to you," Betty rejoined, and then added, "Actually, that looks like a good idea." She decided to have coffee later, and went to the bathroom for a good BM and a long hot bath, which would make her feel better inside and out.

Before lunch she drove to the general store and bought an expensive tomato and a 25-pound bag of Purina Layeena.

"You fixing to raise some chickens?" asked the girl who rang up Betty's purchases.

"No," she answered, and stood with the tomato in her hand, wondering how she was going to get the heavy bag of feed into her car.

"Jesse," the girl said, addressing an old man who was just coming in the door. "Would you carry Miss Reeves' chicken feed out to her car for her?"

"Oh, I reckon," the man answered and bent to scoop the bag onto his shoulder.

"Wait, you can't carry that!" Betty said, but by then the man was holding the door open for Betty to follow him through, his right arm propped on his skinny waist to give the bag of feed a better balance, his light blue eyes peering out from deep crows' feet wrinkles and the shadow of his cap.

Betty walked past him and led the way to the Lincoln. She opened the back door and stood aside while he dropped the bag of feed onto the seat.

"Well, thank you," she said. She knew better than to offer him a tip.

The old man stood with his hands pressed into the back pockets of his jeans, grinning at her. "Been a long time since I seen you buying chicken feed," he said.

"It has?" Betty asked.

"I reckon it's been thirty-five year or more."

"It has?" Betty said again.

"Ain't you Ruben Sells' middle girl Betty, that married Joe Reeves and went off north to live?"

"Who are you?" No need to worry about sounding rude. Prying was what everybody did for entertainment, around here.

"Don't you remember Jesse Edminston? I used to live up at the head of Cleghorn Holler, and run around some with your brother Samuel."

Samuel had been twelve years older than Betty, and had died when his ship was struck by a kamikaze during World War II. She would have sworn she'd never seen this person before in her life.

"Well" she said helplessly, wanting to get back to her double-wide but feeling an obligation to give this old man a few minutes of her time. "How are you?"

Jesse's grin widened. "Best I've ever been!" he said.

Betty looked at his thin, bent frame and mottled hands and thought that if he'd never been better than this, he must have had a long and miserable life.

"You raising chickens?' he asked.

"No, not really." Betty wished people would quit asking her about her interest in poultry. She'd sew her mouth shut with fodder twine before she'd tell anybody about picking up that reject from KFC. "Just one old hen somebody gave me, as a joke. I guess I'll feed it till I can find a home for it."

"Chickens can be right good company. If you pay attention to 'em, you can get to know their personalities. They've got personalities, just like any other animal. And they can get attached to you. Just feed 'em regular, and talk to 'em. They'll get to know you."

"Is that right?" Betty asked with the most disinterest she could squeeze into three words.

"Yeah," he replied, totally missing the implied message. He leaned against the Lincoln's back fender, apparently content to stand and let the day go by.

"I've got to go. Thanks again for carrying the feed." Maybe Jess Edminston had time to loaf, but Betty didn't.

"Uh-huh," Jess said, and he pried himself up from the fender. "Just come go with me."

Betty hadn't heard this standard Highlands County conversation closure in years, and couldn't come up with the proper response. She smiled and nodded at Jesse through the car window, then quickly maneuvered the car onto the road.

As soon as she sprinkled a little of the processed food onto the newspapers in front of the bird, it began making soft clucking sounds and eating, thumping its beak against the newspapers as it gathered the crumbs. Betty watched it clean up every speck. As she poured more food into the box, she said, "Here, I'll give you a little more. Not too much, though. You're not supposed to give a starving man too much to eat, it'll make him sick. You can have some more later."

Betty continued to sit and watch as the bird ate, then sipped from the cup of water, then began to groom itself. After putting a few of its bedraggled feathers to rights, the bird leaned against the side of the box and closed its eyes.

"Yeah, the world has treated you pretty bad, hasn't it?" Betty asked softly. The bird opened one eye, then closed it again. "Been raised by machine, I guess, in a little bitty box in a poultry house somewhere. I remember the chickens we had when I was a girl, how they'd run to catch the potato bugs we'd pick off the vines and throw to them. They used to get in their dusting holes and fluff dirt into their feathers, and lay there like it felt so good. And when I scattered cracked corn for them, they'd run for it like they'd never had such a good thing to eat before.

"We kept a whole flock of chickens, and they'd quarrel and gossip among themselves, just like old ladies. I remember one old black hen, we called her Black Tildy, she used to sneak out and hide a nest of eggs every spring, and hatch some diddles." Betty sat in the Early American-style dining chair that had been part of the furnishings that came with the new doublewide, leaning over the cardboard box and the chicken in it, but her eyes were unfocused, looking at the happenings of another time. The LED clock on the faux marble kitchen counter buzzed on the hour, and brought Betty out of her daydream. Finding herself staring at the chicken huddled asleep on the floor of the box, Betty said, "Well, Tildy, I guess I'm going to have to show you how to be a real chicken. I can't give you to some old farmer who'd put you in with his hens without so much as a hi-dee-ho. The other chickens would peck you to death. So the first thing is, you need to start sleeping on a perch."

Which was easier said than done. Betty looked all through her bright, shining new house, looking for something from which to make a roost, and finally dumped her CD's onto the living room rug. The stand that had held them consisted of two solid wooden ends with three small dowels, about twelve inches long, between them. Betty figured the highest dowel in the stand - the one that had supported the top back corners of the CD's - was high enough off the ground to make Tildy feel like she was really on a roost and yet not too high for the chicken's weak wings to lift her up there. The wooden ends should be heavy enough to support the little hen's slight weight without tipping. Betty put the stand in Tildy's box and sat back to see what would happen.

Nothing happened. Tildy ignored the would-be roost.

Betty left the stand in the box for a whole day without interfering. Then she tried pointing the bird at the roost and giving her a little nudge from behind, to get her going in the right direction. Tildy squawked but didn't offer to scale the mountain.

Then Betty took matters in her own hands, and picked the bird up from the floor of the box and set her on the roost. She positioned Tildy halfway between the two ends, laid her unresisting feet on the dowel, and let go. Tildy thrashed her wings and seemed to skitter on the dowel for a few moments, then fell with a small thump to the floor of the box. She immediately straightened, settled her feathers, and stalked to the opposite corner of the box. From that vantage she glared at Betty so fiercely that Betty retreated to the living room with a cup of coffee.

This situation continued for a week, and then Betty made a trip to the store for a half-gallon of 2% milk and a loaf of wheat bread. Once she got there she strolled casually to the back, where farm supplies were kept, and was standing in front of a row of veterinary supplies when someone behind her said,

"You needing more laying mash already?"

Betty jerked back the hand that had started towards a plastic bottle of all-purpose wormer, and turned to see Jesse Edminston leaning against the ice cream freezer, eating an orange Dreamsicle and grinning at her.

"No, I don't," she replied.

"Well," Jess worked off a bite-sized piece of the Dreamsicle from the part of the stick right above his hand. Without looking at Betty he added, "Chickens don't usually need worming, this time of year."

"I wasn't buying worm medicine, either." Betty frowned at Jess and watched him eating the ice cream as if she were the judge of a neatness contest at the county fair.

Jess smiled briefly. His ice cream was white inside, coated with an orange sherbet-looking layer. Betty could smell it from where she stood. It reminded her of scented candles.

Jess paused again, wiped his mouth with a paper napkin, and asked, without looking at Betty, "Can I buy you a ice cream?"

"No thanks. I was just wondering if..."

Now he did look at her, and she hesitated, hating to give this old man any degree of invitation into her life. Also, she hated to sound like a city-slicker. She had been born and raised here, after all, but it was a long time ago, and things had changed. "I was wondering if there is such a thing as vitamins for chickens. My little hen seems sort of listless."

Jess finished the Dreamsicle, wrapped the napkin around the stick, and dropped them into a metal trash can waiting at the end of the freezer. "Is your chicken setting around with her beak open, gaping?"

"No."

"Does she fall over when she tries to walk?"

"No, but..."

Jess waited patiently, looking straight at Betty without even the suggestion of a smile.

"But you know, it seems like she doesn't walk much. She's never even tried to get out of her box."

"Where'd this chicken come from?"

Betty looked away from Jesse's face, down at his feet in their well-greased leather work boots. She noticed that he wore his dark blue jeans creased and neatly rolled twice at the cuff, probably the exact style he'd worn in 1952. "Well, I... I think she's from one of those poultry houses, where people raise meat market chickens by the thousands."

Jess didn't laugh or move his feet, which were all Betty could see of him, with her face tilted toward the floor. "Let's go take a look," he said, and Betty picked up her bread and milk, paid for them, and went out to the Lincoln. Jess followed without a word, and casually opened the passenger door and slid in. Betty stood for a moment, keys in hand, then shrugged and got in the car. Jess Edminston was so thin and worn, if he tried to pull anything, she knew she could overpower him.

They didn't talk during the ride to Betty's house. She led him in through the back door, and nodded at the box with the chicken in it. He stopped and squatted beside the box while she put the groceries away. Betty started a new pot of coffee and then came to stand beside Jess. "Well?" she said. "What do you think?"

"She's got a right bright eye," he said easily.

"Did you see her walk?" Betty asked.

"No."

"She doesn't walk much. I'm afraid there's something wrong with her feet. She doesn't seem to want to perch, either." Betty was glad her voice sounded casual. She crossed her arms and stood with her weight on one hip.

Jesse reached into the box and picked up the chicken. He held her with his hands under her chest, with her wings under his thumbs. He looked at the chicken's feet, then tucked the bird under his left arm and gently manipulated her claws with his right hand. He smoothed her feathers and set her back in the box, then watched as Tildy shook herself and walked across the box to the cup of water for a drink.

Still with his eyes on the bird, he said, "I don't think there's anything wrong with her feet."

Betty uncrossed her arms.

"I think she's just been kept in a little bitty old cage 'till she don't know how to do much. She's never had the opportunity to walk or fly, nor to scratch in the dirt. She don't hardly know how. You ought to get her out of that box as much as possible, and think of ways to encourage her to walk. She just needs some practice, is what I think."

During this - extraordinarily long, for him, - speech, Jess continued to watch Tildy. Betty thought about what he'd said and then asked,

"Would you like a cup of coffee?"

Jess stood and smiled at her. "I reckon I could handle one." Before Betty turned away, he added, "Is that thing in the corner of her box supposed to be a roost?"

A little too quickly and a little too loudly, Betty answered, "It was just something I had on hand. I thought she'd be more comfortable perching on something."

Without laughing Jess replied, "It may be set too close to the side of the box. Chickens generally like to have a little clearance on all sides when they roost. And she might like a little thicker branch to clamp on to, especially 'till she gets used to it."

"Oh. Well, it was just what I had on hand."

"Yeah."

Betty went to pour coffee.

If anyone had told Betty Reeves that one day she'd let a chicken run loose in her kitchen, and go around wiping up its droppings with paper towels, she'd have suggested that person sign up for a visit with the men in the little white coats. Yet within a week of Jess Edminston's visit, Tildy had the run of the white-and-Williamsburg-blue linoleum in Betty's almost new doublewide mobile home, and Betty kept a roll of cheap paper towels handy. Of course Tildy didn't even try to fly up to the counters - that would have been 'way too much for Betty's sense of sanitation - and she still spent most of her time in the newspapered box. But for a few hours of each day, Betty got Tildy out and, after stroking her feathers a few times, set her in the kitchen floor. At first, Tildy just squatted where she was set, and glared at her owner if Betty happened to be in view.

The whole point of getting the bird out of the box was so she'd practice walking, so Betty tried to talk her into exploring. She coaxed and then argued with Tildy. The bird, somewhat more fully feathered and certainly heavier than when she'd landed on Betty's windshield, was also, if possible, more stubborn. She would appear to listen to Betty for a few moments, then would turn her head away. Betty had never imagined the back of a bird could be so eloquent. Betty began to suspect Tildy had developed the ability to time her manure deposits, because it certainly seemed to happen more when Betty was trying to convince her to get up and move. Then Betty thought of an incentive for the hen. She set Tildy at one end of the narrow kitchen ("galley-style," the brochure called it) and set a jar lid with laying mash in it at the other end. Betty rattled the feed in the lid and said, "Okay, Smarty-Pants, here it is. Come and get it when you're ready."

After an hour during which Tildy had not moved an inch, Betty moved the feed closer to the bird, by half the length of the kitchen. After another half-hour, Betty set the lid eighteen inches from the bird's beak. Tildy looked at the lid and crumbles the way a strong-willed woman might examine an insect, but didn't lift a toe.

Finally Betty set the food right under Tildy's beak, and the hen dug in. After two beakfuls, Betty pulled the dish a few inches away from the bird. Tildy emitted a worried-sounding cluck and scooted forward just enough to reach the feed. Another bite, another removal, just a little farther away.

After several days of this routine, Tildy would get up from her squat in front of the sink and walk across the kitchen floor to get to the feed when Betty rattled it in its pan. As the winter wore on Tildy's legs got stronger, and her sense of proprietary interest developed along with them. She began to wander around the kitchen, giving the cabinet doors intense visual examinations and pecking at specks in the linoleum.

One mid-morning in February when the temperature hadn't risen above nine degrees, Betty was drinking a second cup of coffee and watching the little hen making her rounds of the kitchen when somebody knocked on the back door.

Nobody ever came knocking on Betty's door. She was so startled that for a few seconds she simply sat, looking at the door and wondering who might be out there. It took a second rumble of knocking to get her up, and then she grabbed Tildy and thrust her in the box. Tildy squawked and flapped at the indignity, and continued to mutter imprecations while Betty snatched up the newspapers she had scattered on the kitchen floor, jammed them into the cabinet under the sink, and then went to the door.

She opened it, and there stood Jess Edminston, his skinny form so camouflaged by layers of jackets, vests, coats and caps that he looked to be a much larger man than Betty knew him to be. There was a knitted scarf wrapped around his face from the eyes downward, and the area below the bump of his nose glittered with frozen breath.

Betty looked at Jess in silence.

"Howdy," he finally said. "I thought I might ought to check to make sure you were keeping warm."

Betty blinked, then answered, "I'm fine, thanks."

They stood eyeing each other for several seconds, during which warm air from the doublewide and frigid air from outside exchanged places at breakneck speed. Jess stood on the six-by-six-foot porch with the clear, distant sunlight of winter highlighting all the mismatched pieces of clothing he was wearing.

"How's the little hen?" he asked.

Betty hesitated, then silently stood aside and held the door wider for Jess to enter. He came in quickly.

Jess divested himself of a coat, an insulated vest, a hooded jacket, and two scarves. He laid all these garments, one at a time, on the polished maple table in the dining area. He put a pair of mittens on top of the pile, and a pair of gloves on top of the mittens. He put a knitted cap on top of all. His short, springy gray hair seemed unaffected by all the layers, or by his hands when he ran them over his head. He turned toward Betty and smiled the same, exact smile he'd offered both times she'd met him at the store. Then he walked to Tildy's box and squatted down beside it. Betty followed him.

"Hello, old girl," he said to the hen, speaking softly. Tildy stood up, looked at Jess from each eye, then paraded slowly across her small enclosure. She paused with her back toward Jess and Betty, then craned her head in their direction, and began to groom her already clean, thick feathers.

"Flirt," Betty muttered.

Jess huffed a breathy laugh. "She sure looks better. She's walking good, too."

"I've been giving her some exercise." Betty paused, sniffed. "As you suggested."

"I brought her something." Jess stood and crossed to the table. He sorted through the pile of clothing until he found the pocket of the heaviest coat. From it he pulled a short length of tree branch with the bark still on, nailed at either end to the center of a triangle of milled lumber. "Let's see how this works," he said, and set it in Tildy's box.

Betty watched as Jess murmured to the hen, and stroked her feathers, and gently lifted her. He held her above the branch, and smoothed the hen's toes around it. He supported her for a few seconds, then let go. Tildy sat, both feet firmly clenched around the branch.

Betty held her breath until she saw that the chicken was really sitting on a roost. Just as Betty exhaled, Tildy tilted, flapped, and fell onto the floor of the box. Jess laughed as Tildy gathered herself and stalked back to her favorite corner. Without looking at Betty he said, "I believe she'll get the hang of it, if you'll help her along." He stood up and pushed his hands in his hip pockets, and stood looking down at the bird in her box.

Betty looked at Jess, at his skinny legs and neat boots, at his soft flannel shirt with the cuffs rolled once above the shirt of his long underwear. She sighed and said, "Would you like coffee?"

They sat at the dining table and drank two cups each. Jess told her about his days of working for the state on the highway crew, about the big snows he'd plowed and the times he'd helped repair the washouts when Horse Creek ran out of its banks. She mostly sat and listened, and thought about how quickly she'd gotten used to the Highlands County accent.

He stood up to go, and began to don the layers of his coats and jackets, in proper order and no great haste. "I reckon you've got electric heat in here?" he said.

"That's right."

"I never could get used to it." His voice was softened by the scarf he was wrapping around his face. "I always liked backing up to a wood fire, letting the heat soak in."

"Well, there's no way I could cut wood for a stove. And all that mess, chips and bark dribbling in and ashes dribbling out."

"Yeah," he agreed, and walked to the door. He put his hand on the knob, then turned toward Betty. "If the power ever goes out, I'll check on you."

"I'll be fine, thanks."

Jess looked at Betty for a few seconds, and she thought he might be smiling. At least, the crow's feet around his eyes deepened and stretched. "Just come and go home with me," he said.

But Betty had thought about it, since the first time she'd spoken with Jess Edminston. This time she knew what to say, though she spoke the words without a smile and reluctantly. "Just stay, and I'll fix some dinner."

More wrinkles. "Reckon I'd better get on, check on my chickens. We'll see ya." Jess held up his hand, glove, mitten and all.

"See ya," said Betty, and her hand went up in answer before she thought to keep it still.

In March there was an ice storm. When Betty got out of bed that morning the house felt cold, and she checked the thermostat. It was still set on 72, but the gauge on the bottom read 64. Betty frowned and had the telephone receiver in her hand, ready to call the service department of Billy Bob's Better Homes, when she realized the face of the electric clock was dark. And there was no dial tone. No electricity.

She walked over and looked down into the chicken box. The hen sat on her perch, her feathers fluffed. She tilted her head and looked at Betty with a cheerful glint in her bright, clear eye, apparently waiting for Betty to speak.

"It's a little chilly this morning, isn't it?"

The hen shook her head, then squatted lower, covering her feet more deeply.

Betty walked to the dining area window, pulled aside the lace curtain, then stood in shocked stillness at what she saw. Everything was encased in ice. Every twig, branch, leaf and stem. Every blade of grass, every inch of porch and handrail, every stretch of fence wire was covered, top, bottom and sides. The wires leading to the tall, glittering power pole at the edge of the road were covered in ice too, even though they lay flat on the ground. Over it all shined a bright spring sun, and water was beginning to gather at the edges of eaves and the tips of tree limbs, adding another facet to the diamond effect of sun on ice. It was so quiet that, even from inside, Betty could hear water dripping from the corner of her roof.

Betty's gaze returned to the power lines laying on the ground. "Tildy," she said, "we may be in for trouble."

The hen uttered a long, low cluck, and Betty could tell by the scratch of clawed feet on newspaper that she jumped down from her roost. Despite gaining strength in her feet and legs, Tildy had not shown the least inclination to fly. She got on and off her roost by hopping, and even though she stretched and flapped her wings and groomed them scrupulously, she seemed to be content with life on the ground, or else was disabled in some hidden way.

Betty was relieved that she could keep Tildy in the house and not worry about the bird flapping around and getting on the furniture. She would not admit to herself how much she'd come to rely on the bird for company. It had been harder then she'd expected to re-establish old connections with her childhood friends and family in Highlands County. "These people," as she thought of them, were so old-fashioned. What would her friends in Baltimore have thought of Aunt Josie, who lived in the next house down the road - a cabin, really, covered over with tar paper shingles - and put on a fresh apron every day and wore a bonnet to the garden?

Oh, they were good people, they'd do anything for you, but how could you explain a person like Farm Cregger, who had spent ten years in the pen for making moonshine, and who everybody knew still ran off a batch now and then, right in his wife's kitchen? And ever since he'd had that operation for prostate cancer, he sat right up front in church every Sunday, and nobody said a word about his liquor business.

So Betty stayed home and talked to Tildy. The hen pretty much had the run of the kitchen, dining area and back bathroom now, and sometimes Betty even spread newspapers in the den and let Tildy roam in there. Feeding Tildy twice a day, and changing the newspapers as soon as they were soiled, and washing the floors with Lysol every other day, were routines around which Betty made her days. Her sister, who lived in the old homeplace and still had two children at home as well as a husband who worked a swing shift spraying lacquer at Bailey's furniture factory, called nearly every day, but Betty sometimes felt better understood by the little hen, who listened attentively and never disagreed with Betty's opinions, than by her sister. Shirley seemed to swing between resenting Betty because she'd gone off to the city and prospered, and pitying Betty because she'd gone off to the city and "lost touch." Of course, Betty had also been widowed and raised three sons who'd married city girls and showed no interest in putting roots into Highlands County dirt, so Betty didn't know what Shirley had to be jealous of.

But Betty was nothing if not self-sufficient, so she was polite to Shirley and declined most but not all invitations to dinner at the homeplace, attended the little Methodist church regularly but refused to become involved in committees or issues, and shared her dinners and ideas with Tildy.

This storm, though, could be a real test. Betty wrapped her housecoat more tightly around her chest as she turned away from the window. No electricity meant no heat, no lights, no telephone, no water, no coffee. She decided to put on some warm clothes and drive down to the store. She could use the phone there to notify the power company about the downed lines in front of her house. Maybe they could give her an idea of how long it would take to get power restored.

Betty dressed in slacks, turtleneck pullover, and walking shoes over warm socks. She put some feed out for Tildy, saw that the hen's cup was still half full of water, and opened the back door.

The big E-Z-Read thermometer mounted on the railing showed 34 degrees. After her first glance at its dial Betty looked up, into an alien world of glittering sunlight reflecting off and through a million angles of ice and droplets of water. Betty was dazzled. She hesitated, shielding her eyes with one hand and hanging onto the doorknob with the other.

It was a good thing, too, because when her foot touched the porch floor, it shot out from where Betty had set it as if it had been sent by slingshot. The one foot she had remaining on the un-iced doorstep and her hand on the doorknob became the only stationary points in a world that swung, jumped, glittered, and bounced, until Betty finally settled, clinging grimly, straddle-legged and breathing hard, but basically undamaged.

After a few seconds she drew her feet together on the dry side of the doorway and stood in the shadows, looking out at the Lincoln. It waited with dumb mechanical patience, icicles hanging like fairy chains from its bumper to the ground. Betty realized the car was entombed by ice, completely covered by a bumpy layer nearly an inch thick. Even if she could get to it, she'd have to come up with a way to melt the ice off the door and out of the lock which, despite her sister's derision, she locked every time she exited the car.

She stepped back into the house and shut the door. One thing for sure, she couldn't pour hot water over the Lincoln's door. There was no water to be had, not hot for melting ice or washing hands, or cold for making coffee or flushing the toilet.

And she had been counting on using the restroom at the store to relieve some of that problem, too.

Betty was still standing just inside the back door, unhappily pondering, when she heard a heavy, grinding, clinking noise from outside. She went to the window and looked toward the road. There she saw a vehicle, unidentifiable as to make and model, crawling slowly up the hill. In the distant past some major part of it might have been a pickup, since its front end bore some resemblance to one - or two or three, since there were at least that many colors of paint on it. The original back end had been removed and replaced with a wooden bed without sides, and there were two sets of dual wheels under it. The conglomerate of chassis rode high above the outsized tires, one set of which was wrapped in chains. This caricature of hillbilly transport proceeded at the pace of a dignified walk. Even at that distance Betty could recognize the driver sitting calmly inside the cab, gripping with both hands a steering wheel that was half again wider than he was, gazing straight ahead with pastoral nonchalance.

"Drat," Betty muttered.

She continued to watch until the truck turned into her driveway and crawled up behind the Lincoln. She saw Jess Edminston fiddle with gear sticks and the brake lever, then start to open the truck door.

Betty hurried across the dining area and flung open her own door. "Stop," she yelled. "Stop right there."

Jess paused, standing on the running board, one hand on top of the open truck door and the other still grasping the steering wheel. "Morning, Betty," he yelled back. "I've come to take you to my house." The truck's motor was still running, rumbling in a deep and steady throb.

Betty snorted, but not loudly enough for Jess to notice. "I'm not going anywhere, and you're not setting foot on the ground here. If either one of us tried, we'd break a bone or maybe two or three, and then we'd really be up the creek. You go on home."

Jess stood on the edge of his pieced-together truck and looked at her. Finally he called, "You don't have any power. The lines are down, right here and all over."

"Well, there's a news flash," Betty said to Tildy. "That's right!"

she shouted out the door. "Why don't you go report my power outage? I'll be fine." After a two-second pause, she added. "Thank you."

Jess continued to stand on his truck in her driveway, silent, his face aimed in her direction. Finally Betty waved at him, retreated through the doorway, and shut it behind her. Maybe he'd get the idea. Anyway, she couldn't afford to stand there with the door open. It might be 34 and thawing outside, but that was a long way below the temperature inside, and she didn't want the two evening out any more than she could help. It might be hours before the line was repaired and the heat came back on. She didn't want Tildy to get chilled.

It was almost four days before the work crews pulled in from across the region by Appalachian Power could get all the lines repaired and power fully restored. Temperatures dropped to below freezing during the first night, and stayed there. Ice on the roads stayed too, making it difficult for crews to follow the lines across the county. In Betty's community, only a very few vehicles could maneuver the slick roads. Jess Edminston had one of them.

When the motley truck pulled into her driveway for the second time, at 9:20 (according to Betty's wristwatch) on the second morning without power, Betty went to the door and waited for Jess to get close enough for communication.

The truck stopped, Jess fiddled with gears, then he opened his door and stuck his head above it. "Morning," he said calmly. "Just thought I'd stop and say howdy. I reckon you're just fine?"

Betty couldn't hear even a hint of sarcasm in his tone. "Yes, I'm just fine. Do you know when the power will be back on?" In spite of herself, she couldn't keep a note of concern out of her own voice. Tildy was out of water, and the little hen was staying on her roost this morning, fluffed to maximum proportions.

"They're saying Tuesday, maybe."

Betty bit her bottom lip.

Jess paused politely, but when Betty didn't respond, he cheerfully asked, "How's the little hen?"

Betty was relieved to be able to express some of her concern. "I'm getting worried. She's never been in the cold. Do you think she'll take a chill?"

Jess appeared to consider this seriously. "Is she eating good?"

"Seems to me like she may have slacked off a little, today and yesterday."

"She getting plenty of water?"

"Well, to tell you the truth," Betty hesitated, then, for Tildy's sake, admitted, "we're out of water in here."

Jess didn't change his posture or tone. He let his gaze travel idly over the house and yard. "I could carry in some water for you, a little drinking water for you and Tildy, and enough to flush the commode a time or two."

"When?"

"I got a couple of five-gallon buckets right in the truck, here."

Betty didn't think about it long. She'd had no choice but to use the commode, and she wanted to flush nearly as badly as she wanted coffee. And Tildy needed a drink. "Be careful walking over here," she said. "It's still solid ice."

He gave her a small salute, then went back into the truck and turned off the engine. Betty watched through the window while Jess walked carefully around the front of the truck, holding onto the bumper, then opened the passenger door and lifted out a metal bucket with a handle but no lid. He scattered material from this bucket in front of his feet as he walked slowly up the side of her driveway to the porch steps. He set the bucket down and hollered, "Betty. Oh, Betty Louise!"

When she opened the door and looked down at Jess, he asked if she might have a shovel on the place. She went to the coat closet and came back with a folding camping shovel that she'd used to dig holes to set out some rose bushes, in the fall. She pushed it across the porch floor to him, and he thanked her and then set to chopping lightly at the icy coating on the steps. He worked steadily if not speedily, and when he had cleared a narrow path up the steps and to the door, he went back and brought the bucket, scattering it's contents in his cleared path.

Then he went back to the truck and brought out a large plastic bucket with a snap-on lid. As he approached the door, Betty held it wide open, then hurried to get in front of him and led the way to the bathroom. She set the lid off the tank and he poured water from the bucket in and, almost before he was through pouring, she pushed the handle. She listened to the swoosh and gurgle with gratitude.

He went back to the truck and traded the empty bucket for a full one, which he carried to the bathroom and set in the tub, then made another trip and came back with two gallon milk jugs filled with water. He handed these to her and while she filled Tildy's cup he unzipped his coat. They both watched the hen drink, then hop back onto her perch and squat.

"Do you think she's cold?" Betty asked.

"She might be. Like you said, she's not used to weather." There was some minutes' pause before Jess offhandedly inquired, "Can't you go down and stay with Shirley for a couple of days?"

"They're pretty crowded, down there. And she'd never let a chicken into her house." She didn't add that she'd never in a million years ask her sister to treat a chicken like a pet. How pathetic she would seem, and full of city notions.

Jess didn't comment. Soon he said, "I reckon I'll get on." He zipped his coat and turned toward the door, and Betty was surprised by a momentary rush of desire for him to stay. She said, "I'd offer you coffee if I had any way to fix it."

He smiled at her, and offered that oh-so-useful phrase, "Well." He went to the door and turned the knob, but before he'd opened it even a crack, he said, without facing her, "You and the hen both would be welcome to come to my house for a while. It's warm, and I could fix a little bite of something to eat." This was an entirely different offer from the ritualized invitations he'd extended before.

"You have heat?"

He turned and grinned. "Big wood stove. Dirty, but it keeps goin'. Wood stove in the kitchen too, an old Knox Mealmaster. Best cooking stove there is."

Betty gnawed at her lip, then looked in the box and said, "What do you think, Tildy? Want to go visit Mr. Edminston?"

Jess looked in the box, too. "Guess what, Tildy? There's a hand pump in a little room right off the kitchen. Heat and water."

Betty could have sworn there was a special gleam in the hen's eye as she hopped off her roost. She chuckled and Jess laughed outright.

Betty found a tomato box with a lid (she'd been secretly saving it, in case she needed to carry Tildy to the vet's) and installed Tildy in it. Jess carried it to the truck carefully, while Betty walked behind them, holding onto any steady thing that came close enough to the path Jess had made. The mixture of fine gravel and rock salt he'd scattered on the ground provided fairly good footing, and all three members of the party made it to their transport without incident. The hardest part was getting Betty into the cab of the truck, which was higher than she'd imagined. She finally was able to crawl in, after declining Jess' offer of a boost from behind, by putting one foot on the running board, pushing off with the other foot, and pulling with both hands grabbing the plastic seat covers.

After that, the drive to Jess' house was anticlimactic. Jess paid strict attention to the road. Betty wondered how big her rear had looked to Jess, who'd insisted on standing directly behind her while she struggled into the truck, "in case she fell," and worried about how Tildy was getting along in her box. She held her leather-gloved hands tightly clasped, so she wouldn't lift the lid and peek in, like a kid with a new puppy.

To Betty's surprise, Jess drove down the mountain and past her old homeplace. "I thought you lived in Cleghorn Holler?" she said.

"No, I said I used to live there. When I was a kid. I bought the old MacMillan place years ago."

While Betty was trying to remember where the MacMillan place was, Jess steered the truck off the highway and onto a graveled lane that led upward. They drove through a pasture field, crossed a small, dark creek, and passed through a grove of stern hemlock trees. Finally they emerged onto a gently sloping shelf of open land backed by a much steeper bank of deciduous trees whose fingertips were beginning to show buds. Pressed into the wooded bank was a white farmhouse. Its exposed foundation was narrow at the back but shoulder high under the front porch, and at either end of the house the laid stones rose up to form wide, gray chimneys. A thin spiral of white smoke curled above one of these.

Jess drove the truck past the front of the house and pulled up to a back door. He fiddled with the gears, turned off the engine, and set a hand brake before he slid out of the truck. Betty pushed hard against her door, hurrying so he wouldn't have any excuse to try to help her out, and by the time he'd crossed from his side of the truck to hers, she was picking herself up from the yard. She stood quickly, and turned to reach back into the truck for Tildy's box. Maybe if she pretended she hadn't scooted right off that plastic seat onto the wet dead grass and mud, on her hands and knees, he would pretend he hadn't seen it happen.

Obligingly, he said, "Let me carry that box."

She stood on tiptoe and leaned as far inside the truck as she could, and was barely able to snag the handle hole of the box with one finger. She dragged it to the edge of the seat, lifted it out, and carefully handed it to Jess. He turned and she followed him through the screened back door, across a small enclosed porch that was nearly filled with stacked firewood, and into the house through a smallish, solid wood door.

As soon as she stepped inside, Betty was washed over by warmth and a heavy blend of odors. She hadn't realized how cold she was. The heat felt like heaven.

Jess walked directly to a big, heavy-looking stove. He set Tildy's box in the floor, then lifted part of the top of the stove and looked in. He moved between the stove and a nearby woodbox while Betty looked at his kitchen.

It was a large room, low-ceilinged and dark, with one window opening onto the porch and another, over the sink, shadowed by an evergreen tree and the wooded hillside, which, on this back side, met the house's knees. Formica counters with cabinets above and below them filled the entire wall around the double sink, but that was the only modern concession in the room. The wood stove sat firmly ensconced against the wall Betty was facing, claiming its place with weight and dignity. Near it was a wooden rocking chair with a floor lamp in attendance; beyond them lurked a huge wooden dresser. Betty could barely see the gleam of dishes behind the glass-paned doors on the upper half of the cabinet. There was mild clutter on top of the base cabinet, papers and maybe envelopes, a stack of magazines, some pieces of wood piled together, a portable radio.

One half of the room was given over to a wooden table big enough to seat ten or twelve people. Along one side - beneath the porch window - was a bench. At either end and on the opposite side, an assortment of wooden chairs was poised. Betty had a sudden vision of the table covered with food: a whole turkey on a platter with dressing bulging out its front and back ends, steaming bowls of potatoes and green beans, gravy in a small pitcher, sweet potatoes with little marshmallows baked to golden brownness on top, ham, and butter in a china dish set ready next to a plate of stacked biscuits, high, bumpy, tanned, and tender.

Betty hadn't made biscuits from scratch in years. When the boys were little, they'd clamored to have the store-bought kind, that came in a cardboard tube and could be swallowed in two bites. Her momma, though, had baked biscuits twice a day, cutting lard into self-rising flour with a fork, dumping the dough onto her breadboard and giving it three or four thumps to flatten it, and sliding the pan into her wood stove with a clatter and a slam. Betty was suddenly hungry for those biscuits, hot and brown, moist on the inside.

Jess had finished stoking the stove, and he'd turned and caught Betty staring at the table. Embarrassed, she asked, "You feed a lot of people in here?"

"Not reg'lar." he said. "Why don't you take your coat off and stay a while?"

Betty took off her coat, and Jess hung it with his own on a multi-hooked coat tree beside the door. Then he said he needed to check the fire in the other stove, and asked if she'd like to see the rest of the house. They walked down a short central hall, and Jess turned right, into the living room, where a smaller stove crouched on the old hearth. A small room with three walls of windows had been added to the front of the house, and a doorway to it had been cut through the living room's front wall, with three or four steps leading down to it. A bathroom opened off a back corner.

Across the hall from the living room was Jess' bedroom, shown briefly, and upstairs were two bedrooms, each with an iron bed dressed in quilts, linoleum with pictures of overblown roses on the floors, and not much else.

The living room, window room and bathroom were heated by the stove in the living room and were warm enough. Except for the doors connecting those three rooms, all the interior door were kept closed, and the rest of the house was cold.

"Don't you mind sleeping in the cold?" Betty asked.

"No, it's the way I was raised. It's the only way I sleep good. I like the weight of a quilt," he answered.

Betty thought of her own bed, made up with an ultra-light electric blanket and polished cotton sheets, and shivered. The night before she had searched for extra blankets to use while the power was out, and had finally thrown her good winter coat over the bed, too.

"I smell the coffee," Jess said, and they went back into the kitchen.

He wouldn't let Betty do anything, but installed her in the rocking chair, and told her to watch Tildy. The hen was taken out of her box and told to "check out this new place." She strolled about on the newspapers Jess spread around the floor, pecking and looking, holding her head with a lift and tilt that indicated an attitude that Betty said was arrogant and Jess thought was "queenly." Betty smiled, although she would never have said such a thing, herself.

Betty sat near the stove, feeling the heat seep into her deep parts, loosening joints and relaxing a knot she hadn't known was in her stomach. Jess bustled in and out of the "pump room," built at a lower level than the kitchen to take advantage of the earth's insulation. Here there was a concrete trough along one wall with a hand pump at one end, where deep well water was available even when the power was off, and shelves were full of canned vegetables and meats.

"Do you do your own canning, too?" Betty demanded, when he showed her the room.

"No. I make a big garden every year, and take the stuff to my sister, and she cans it for both of us. We butcher a hog every year. And she cans some chicken and rabbit for me."

"Rabbit!"

"Lord, yes. Canned rabbit is some of the best eating there is."

Betty held her tongue, but swore to herself that she'd not eat any unidentified meat that Jess prepared.

Soon he was filling two plates from pots on the stove, and he told her to come to the table. She left the rocker with some reluctance, thinking of Jess'es canned rabbit, but when he asked how long it had been since she'd had gravy and pork tenderloin, she was reassured. She sat at the end of the big table, and Jess sat at her right hand. He had already put glasses of water at their places, and now he said, "Well, it ain't fancy, but it's hot. Tell me what you think."

Betty took up a fork and cut a small piece from the chunk of pale meat on her plate. Jess had cooked it in gravy made from the juices in the can, and it was speckled with black pepper and rich with canned milk. When she put it in her mouth, the meat fell into shreds.

"It's delicious!" Betty didn't think until too late that it was rude to sound so surprised, but Jesse didn't seem to take offense. He smiled at her, then dropped his gaze to his own plate.

Not only was the pork and gravy good, but the green beans were savory, and the applesauce was thick and not too sweet, the way Betty liked it. Best of all were the biscuits. She had watched Jess mixing the dough and patting it out. He had cut out the biscuits using a tin can with one end removed and holes punched in the other end. It looked to Betty like an evaporated milk can, and it cut large circles of dough that grew even larger in the oven. "Cat-head biscuits," Jess called them, and when she raised her eyebrows at him, he briefly explained, "Big as a cat's head." Betty ate one with gravy, one plain with butter, and a third with butter and honey.

Afterwards, Betty helped Jess wash the dishes, using water heated in a big aluminum kettle on the stove. Jess gave Tildy some laying mash and cracked corn, mixed, on a paper plate, and then put her back in her box.

Betty and Jess went to the living room. Betty stood near the stove and looked at the pictures propped on the mantle and hung on the wall around the fireplace.

"Who's this?" she asked, looking at an Olin Mills portrait of three children.

"My sister Janelle's kids. That was made some years ago. That oldest one, he's married and has two kids of his own, now. They live in Marion." He stood at her side and pointed to each of the pictures, identifying sisters and brothers, nieces and nephews, cousins and old friends. There was a picture of his mother and father, made in 1969, and another of his mother, taken just before her death in 1995, at the age of 97.

"Ninety-seven. Imagine living to be so old," Betty said.

"She lived with me for the last five years of her life. Her mind was clear as mine, right to the end."

"How did she die?"

"Just got tired one day. She'd picked a big mess of green beans that morning, and set down to break them. When I come in for dinner, I saw the bag of beans and the dishpan that she'd started breaking them into, setting on the table. I went to her room and she was laying on her bed with a quilt over her legs. I went in and said, 'Mommy, are you feeling bad?' 'I'm just a little tired, son,' she said. 'I believe I'll rest a while.' But it was so unlike her to lay down in the middle of the day, I knew something was wrong. I loaded her into the truck and took her to the doctor. She said Mommy's heart was beating real slow, hardly going at all, and said we should take her to the hospital.

"But Mommy wouldn't hear of it. She always was a sweet woman, but hard as stone when she made her mind up about something. And she'd made up her mind about this. She said for me to take her home, and let her rest in her own bed, and so I did. I brought her back here and called all the family, and all of them came that could. And the doctor came up a little later, and said Mommy wasn't in pain and would likely go easy.

"She mostly slept, and would wake every once in a while and say hello to whoever was sitting with her. She knew everybody, right to the end, and was cheerful. And you know what the last thing she said was?"

"No, what?"

"She said, 'Jesse, I see a spiderweb a-hangin' in that corner. Go get the broom, son, and let's rake it out, for I hate to show a dirty house to your daddy when he comes.' And then just in a few minutes she was gone. Peaceful and easy. Daddy'd been gone twenty-one years, and she was still eager for him to come home."

Betty stood in the glow of heat from the stove, looking at the picture of Jesse's mother, and remembered her husband's death. "When Joe died, they had him on life support for four days. Tubes taped in his mouth, and his nose, and... I finally told them to turn it off."

"What'd he die of?"

"Complications of emphysema. Diabetes. His circulation was so bad, his feet got infected and they amputated them two years before he died. The funeral home tried to charge me for socks and shoes to bury him in."

Betty had been outraged by the charges on the itemized list provided by Morley Funeral Service. And she had been ashamed to have to confront the people at Morley's, with their soft, shaded lighting and deep carpets, but she had had to. Had to.

Throughout Joe's last years, Betty had dealt with the indignities of his diseases. She had struggled daily, almost hourly, to spare Joe the torture of having others see the effects of them on his body. The cruel claws of diabetes had crawled through Joe, slowing circulation and debilitating organs. Emphysema froze his lungs, so breathing was harder work for Joe then he had ever done for Bethlehem Steel. Those were bad enough, and then doctors had done things to Joe that were horrible. Betty had sometimes felt that the treatments were almost as bad as the diseases.

And to have gone through all that and taken care of Joe as best she could, and then to have had to confront those falsely solicitous and unctuous funeral people because they charged her for shoes and socks for Joe's poor footless body!

Jesse laughed.

Betty whirled to stare at him. He stood grinning at her, smiling in the face of her old shame and anger.

Before she could gather her energies enough to form words, Jess said, "I guess you straightened them out!"

Betty stood, openmouthed but unable to speak.

"Knowing Betty Sells, I'd say you reamed them out good."

"Actually," Betty said slowly, "Actually, I did."

Jesse laughed again. "I'll bet you made some faces red."

Betty remembered the pretty young woman behind the desk, perfectly coiffured and made up, her nails lacquered to exactly match her lipstick, whose face had flushed red and then paled. "Yeah, I guess I did." Betty felt a small smile creeping out from behind the wall of her old pain. "They gave me a real deal on that funeral, too." She'd never told anybody that, before. It had always shamed her. She hadn't set out to bargain on the price of Joe's funeral, but they had insisted on a big discount, a token of their regret, they'd said, over the mix-up.

Jess hooted. He walked across the room and sat down on the couch. "I remember that time when you was in about the fifth grade, and that teacher, what was his name? Hopkins? Haskins? Halsey? Something, anyway, he had that littlest Joines boy up in front of the class, raggin' on him because he had come to school dirty. And up you jumped and lit into that teacher about how they was poor and his momma was down in the bed sick. I'll never forget that as long as I live."

Betty stood and warmed her hands. Jess sat easily, evidently content to let the silence flow around them. Finally Betty pulled an upholstered rocker closer to the stove, and sat, too. The stove pinged and inside it the fire mumbled and growled to itself. Betty became aware of the wind whispering around a corner of the old house and playing in the bare limbs of the trees behind the house. After a while Jess got up and left the room. Betty heard the distant sounds of the kitchen stove being stoked, and Jess speaking to Tildy, and then he came back and sat down again. Betty began to rock a little, letting the rockers hiss against the floor.

"Nobody's called me Betty Sells in a long, long time," she said, looking through the doorway of the window room, into the bright, cold day outdoors.

"It's still your name, ain't it?"

"Everybody who's known me in the last thirty-five years has known me as Betty Reeves. Joe's wife. Terry's mother, Billy's mother, Buddy's mother. Nobody knew about Betty Louise Sells."

They allowed a long silence to grow around them. Betty rocked and looked through the window room. Jess locked his hands together behind his head. He dozed a little, woke, rose to stoke the stove on the hearth and the kitchen stove again. When he came back from the kitchen, Betty stirred and said, "You'd better take me back to my house, Jess."

He pushed his hands into his hip pockets and looked at her sternly. "It's going to be cold in your house."

"Yes it is, but I'll be fine."

"What'll you do for light?"

"If you'll stop at the store I'll get some fresh batteries, and I can use my flashlight when I need to."

"Huh. Store's been out of batteries since yesterday."

"I'll be okay. I need to get back to my place."

He looked at her sharply for a few seconds, and she returned his look evenly. "What about Tildy?" he asked.

Now her eyes fell, and she took a deep breath. "I was wondering if she could stay with you for the night. I hate to ask. I wouldn't, if I could think of any other place I could put her, and keep her warm."

"Okay," he said.

She didn't look up. "I know it's an awful imposition. It's crazy, keeping a chicken in the house like this, and I never intended for it to happen. One thing led to another and I couldn't just let her die-"

"It's okay."

"People will think I've lost my marbles, trying to make a pet out of a factory chicken -"

"Betty."

She stopped talking.

"Betty?"

She looked at him, frowning, jaws clamped.

"I'll be glad to keep your little hen for the night. It's no trouble. You don't think she's the first animal that's spent the night in that kitchen, do you?"

Betty glared at him.

"Orphaned lambs, pups, kittens and old cats. I can't tell you how many boxes of baby rabbits my nieces and nephews have brought in from the fields and tried to raise. Lord, once one of 'em had an old bird cage with a rat in it. Now, Mommy didn't like that one at all."

"Are you sure?"

"She's not even the first chicken. We used to order day-old chicks fifty at a time, slide the whole box of 'em right under the stove."

"I could come back early tomorrow, and clean up after her."

Jess opened the door into the hallway. "You come back tomorrow. Cleaning up after Tildy is no problem."

In the kitchen, Jess handed Betty her coat, then told her to wait a minute while he got the truck started. While he was gone Betty checked on Tildy, who seemed content in her box near the stove. "Well, behave while I'm gone. Don't carry on with Jess. He's a little old for you."

Tildy cocked her head and gave Betty a one-eyed yet meaningful look, then began to preen her breast.

"Yes, I know. He treats you like a queen. But you just remember who saved you from the McNuggets factory."

The hen stilled, shook her head, then stretched out one claw and began to nip off nonexistent mites.

Betty smiled and straightened just as Jesse came for her.

It was a long night in the new double-wide. Betty couldn't seem to get warm, though she had every blanket, afghan and coat she owned, draped on the bed. She'd discovered several candles in the drawer with the good silverware, and had tried to read a paperback romance by their light, but found that if she sat close enough to the grouped candles to be able to see the small print, she was in constant danger of setting her hair on fire. She was uneasy about the candles anyway, and kept moving them from place to place, trying to find one that was perfectly impervious to both ignition and hot wax damage. Finally she gave up and extinguished them all except the scented one shaped like a lotus blossom that floated on blue-tinted water in a brandy snifter on the back of the commode. From her position in her bed, propped up on three pillows and held down by the layers of blankets and clothing, she could see its very pale light filtering into the darkness of the hallway.

She was still awake when the bathroom candle burned itself out, and then she lay in total darkness. Betty thought it was the deepest, blackest darkness she had ever experienced. In Baltimore there had been street lights, and security lights on the eaves of people's garages. There had been a general glow reaching up from the city and reflected downward by muggy nighttime air, which provided at least a means of identifying your location. Of course those lights were shut out of Betty's house by heavy draperies and shades and venetian blinds, but there had been nightlights in the children's rooms and bathrooms, and the green shine of digital electric clocks in her bedroom, and even the glow provided by the power buttons of the VCR, television and cable box in the living room.

But this! This was utter, pitchy blackness. This was almost unendurable. This was darkness compounded by loneliness, this was darkness as complete as the nighttime of the grave, and Betty felt entombed, shrouded by the heavy covers and casketed by the blackness. Suddenly she could bear it no longer, and she flailed her arms wildly, trying to push the heavy coats and blankets away; she struggled to reach the side of the bed and kicked against the clinging heaps of bedclothes. She shoved and grunted and wriggled until suddenly she landed with a thud on the carpet. She reached out wildly and grabbed something, whatever came into her hand, and pulled hard against it, to lever her body up from this deep, dark pit.

With a rip and a clatter, the bedroom curtains (part of the coordinated furnishings chosen by someone at Billy Bob's Better Homes - perhaps even by Bob himself,) tumbled down onto Betty's head. This new assault by the Forces of Fabric might have put Betty right over the edge into total hysteria, but their removal from the window allowed a sudden shaft of moonlight to knife into the room, and when Betty jerked the heavy cotton off her head, she could see.

She sat, panting, and locked her eyes onto the rectangle of brighter darkness, speckled with a few tiny stars, that hung before her face. "Jesus," she whispered.

When she got her wind back, Betty put her hand against the wall for support, and stood up. She pressed her face against the window and looked out at an un-electrified world.

A three-quarter moon sailed serenely above the unconnected power pole out front. Frost glittered like fairy dust. The bright silvery light seemed not to cast shadows, but the world stopped at the edges of things. Tonight, you either lived in the cold moonlight or were cast into the unlife of Stygian blackness.

Betty closed her eyes for a minute. The moonlight almost hurt them. She turned away from the window, and when she opened them again, she recognized her good coat tangled in the pile in the floor. She pulled it out and put it on, and felt her way down the hall. In the living room, she impatiently pushed at the drapes hanging over the largest window, until she could look out again.

The world spread out from her front yard like a blanket, tossed and snapped before settling on an unmade bed. Ridge after ridge of forests and pasture, embroidered with the fancy stitches of fencerows, stacked hay, and power poles, lay before her. The air was so clear and details so sharp that Betty could see the cows gathered around the hay scattered in G. H. Sharpe's pasture, four ridges distant. She could see two or three farmhouses, nestled in the high ends of hollers, and she could see scraps of the highway as it cut back and forth from shoulder to cove, on its way to busier places.

And in all the acres of farm and forest, along the highway and in the houses, not a single hint of modern humanity showed. The houses might have been the cabins of settlers, with heavy log walls and stout doors locked with sliding bars. At all the houses Betty could see, thin white slivers of smoke slid from chimneys. The hardtop highway was transformed by moonlight into an older, dirt path, running at an Indian's pace along a traditional way. No car or truck sliced away the illusion, no artificial light shut out the moon- and star-light.

Betty stood and stared until she began to feel cold. Then she went back to her bedroom, pulled a blanket from the tangled mess, and returned to the living room. She curled up in the corner of the couch, wrapped the doubled blanket around her, and propped her head against one of the decorator pillows - which had never before been evicted from its tasteful position in the matching wing chair - so she could see out. For the rest of the night Betty looked at moon-light, and mountains, and twinkly stars in a sky that was black but not dark.

When Jesse came to pick her up the next morning, she was

ready. He didn't even have time to get out of the truck before she was walking down the porch stairs. She was carrying an overnight bag, and she smiled and waved at him to stay in the truck. She opened the passenger door and crawled in, and he backed out her driveway before he glanced at her and asked, "Did you have a good night?"

Betty looked straight ahead and considered his question. "I got along all right," she eventually answered. "Jess, would you mind taking me to my sister's house, instead of to your place, this morning?"

"That'ud be no trouble."

"Thank you." Betty released a held breath. "How's Tildy?"

"Fine as frog's hair. That's as pretty a little hen as you could ask for. Keeps herself all neat and straightened."

"I hope it won't be too much of an imposition on you, if I have to ask you to keep her for another day or two. Until the power comes back on. I'm thinking about staying with Shirley, if she'll let me."

"No problem." Jess kept his eyes on the road and didn't ask why or how come. For which Betty was grateful.

June 2 was a beautiful early summer day, a kind of day that Betty had forgotten existed. In Baltimore, the weather had always seemed to jump from cold and sleety straight into hot and muggy; from crocuses blooming through wet snow to fighting with the boys to get the lawn mowed. Here, spring and summer were on friendlier terms, and worked together to make a time of bright, warm days and cool nights. It was good weather for peas and spinach and slim new onions. And it made the little fire she had in the woodstove for cooking supper every night, feel delicious.

It had taken much less time and trouble to switch houses with Shirley than Betty had feared it would. As soon as she'd convinced Shirley she was serious and wasn't suffering from Alzheimer's or some other form of dementia, Shirley wasted no time informing her husband and daughters that they were moving.

Betty suggested they take whatever was of personal value from the house, and leave the rest. She'd taken only her clothing from the doublewide, plus some boxes from Baltimore she'd never unpacked. Of the things Shirley left, Betty gave some away and threw some away and kept a little. She was buying a piece of furniture now and then, as she saw one she liked and could afford, mostly from used furniture stores or junk shops. Furniture in her new old house wasn't gong to match, and there wasn't gong to be more of it than she needed. And there were no curtains on any of the windows.

When Betty heard a vehicle approaching, she looked out the kitchen window to make sure it was Jess. He pulled his little pickup into its usual spot beside the Lincoln, and Betty recognized the squeak as he set the hand brake. She wiped her hands and draped the towel over the stove's warming shelf before she went out.

"You're right on time," she said as he got out of the truck. He smiled in reply. He walked to the back of the truck and lifted out a big cardboard box. Betty walked beside him to a small outbuilding in her back yard. There was a large wire pen attached to one side of the outbuilding, with a gate in one side. He knelt and used his pocket knife to cut the twine holding down the flaps of the box, then held the box shut with one hand while he pushed open the gate with the other.

"All right, girls. Try this on for size." He held the box inside the pen and gently tilted it. Eight young chickens strolled out, clucking and clicking, shaking down their feathers and scratching themselves. They spread across the grassy floor of the pen and began to peck and claw at the dirt. Jess pulled the gate closed.

"They seem to think it will do," Betty said, watching the birds.

"It's a fine pen."

"Let's just hope everyone agrees." Betty walked to the building to which the fence of the pen was attached, and opened the door. She walked up the three wooden steps, and spoke in a cheerful voice. Then she came out, holding Tildy comfortably under her arm.

Tildy had grown into a beautiful hen, with thick feathers as richly white as Jersey milk. She wore a beautiful red comb as if it was a fine French chapeau, and looked at the world with a saucy glint in her golden eyes. She was the nearest thing to a lap chicken there ever had been, and would stay in the new chicken house Jess and Betty had built for her only if they took her out to it after dark and placed her claws on the roost when she was dopey with the evening. Otherwise she clucked and squawked to be let out and made it clear that she considered the kitchen to be her personal domain.

Jess opened the gate again, and Betty gently set Tildy inside. He closed the gate and Betty stood with her fingers on the latch, poised to rush in and rescue her chicken, if the newcomers tried too aggressively to establish a pecking order.

For a few minutes, all the chickens in the pen seemed to be oblivious of each other. Tildy, plump and fastidious, sat preening her glossy feathers while the others eagerly searched the grass. Then one of the brown pullets came close to Tildy, walking slowly in a one-claw-at-a-time style. She cast surreptitious glances at Tildy and circled closer and closer, while Tildy ignored her and worked on her left wing feathers.

"Look at that hussy," Betty whispered.

"Which one?" Jess asked.

Betty didn't answer, but drew in a hissing breath as the brown hen stopped walking and stood just inches from Tildy, gazing pointedly in the opposite direction. The slim bird uttered a long, inquisitive cluck, then quickly turned her head. The two birds were nearly beak to beak.

Tildy seemed to become aware of the newcomer all at once. She froze. Then the brown hen turned her head from side to side, checking with each eye, clucking conversationally. Another of the pullets was coming closer, pretending nonchalance while circling in.

"Jess..." Betty whispered.

Jess stood at his ease, hands in his hip pockets, watching.

Then Tildy squawked in a rather unladylike fashion, threw out her wings and stepped back. She turned her head away from the brown hen, and in the instant, the hen stretched out her neck and pecked Tildy in the center of her back.

"Jess!" Betty yelled, but her voice was drowned by the shrieks Tildy emitted. "Grab her, quick!" Betty snatched Jesse's arm as though she was going to sling him through the gate to her pet's rescue, but Jess stood firm. "Hurry, help her!" Betty urged.

Inside the pen, hysteria spread from one chicken to another with the speed of gossip. All the young hens were racing from place to place, turning abruptly, backtracking, running into each other, and all of them were screeching and flapping. Two of them hit upon the idea of flinging themselves against the wire fencing, and one clung there, her claws firmly clenched in the mesh, her wildly flapping wings releasing little feathers that whirled in the drafts created by her flailing pinions. The other was unable to get a purchase on the fence, and so threw herself against it repeatedly while spewing a stream of poultry profanity that needed no translating.

In the midst of this madness, Tildy stood on her tiptoes, wings spread, twisting her head to see all the antics taking place around her. Her beak hung open and she blinked rapidly, clearly unable to comprehend her place in the midst of this hell. Suddenly one crazed pullet, which had been circling in the outside lane of the pen at ever-increasing speeds and who was approaching launch velocity, miscalculated the northwest curve, came down the straight-away two degrees too much to the inside, and plowed into Tildy's rear.

Tildy screamed, jumped, and flailed her wings with all the power that six months of high-grade laying mash and continual pampering could produce.

Betty and Jess watched, in shocked silence, as Tildy rose above the maddened pullets, teetered briefly in midair, then began to fly towards the old cherry tree standing between the hen house and the garden. In the pen, the young chickens got tired and quit scaring themselves, and Betty and Jess could plainly hear Tildy's beautiful, perfectly feathered wings, fanning strongly. She landed clumsily on the cherry's lowest branch and then balanced awkwardly while she turned around and squatted on the branch. From this vantage point, Tildy gazed over the new pen as if she'd sat upon tree branches all her life.

Betty closed her eyes, brought to view on the backs of her eyelids the scene she had just witnessed. She saw Tildy on tiptoe, wings flapping, then rising from the sweet spring grass. She saw the strong white wings against the sapphire sky, the dazzling depth of color in the new leaves of the cherry tree, and the power in the bird's wings.

Betty turned to Jess and said, "She flew."

"Yeah."

"I didn't think she could."

"I figured she would, when she got ready. She's feisty enough."

They both looked at the white hen, sitting now at ease, straightening some feathers on her breast.

"Do you think she'll know enough to come down?" Betty murmured.

"Yeah."

"Do you think she'll ever get along with the other chickens?" By now Betty was so used to Jesse's short answers and long silences, she didn't really expect him to answer. After several more minutes, Jess went into the hen house and came out with a small dishpan with a mixture of cracked corn and laying mash in it. He opened the gate in the fenced pen, stepped inside, and began slowly to scatter the feed around his feet and to hold a quiet conversation with the chickens. The young hens gathered near him, scratching and pecking and murmuring back to him. The madness of fifteen minutes before might have happened to a whole other set of birds. From her place on the cherry branch, Tildy watched.

After few seconds, she rose to her feet, sat back down, then rose again. She stood and watched as Jess scattered the last of the feed, stepped back through the gate and closed it behind him. Tildy muttered anxiously, sat down, stood up, flapped her wings. Then she jumped off the limb and with a few flaps to get her going, sailed into the pen. Her landing was more utilitarian than graceful, but it put her next to a place where the corn lay thick among the stalks of grass. She stood, shook herself down, and began to eat. Soon she was casually working among the other hens, muttering and digging.

"You'd think she'd lived with other chickens all her life." Betty's voice held just a touch of fond disgust.

"Well, she has. For a long time she had thousands of chickens all jammed up around her, but she wasn't able to touch them. You might say she had no relationship with any of 'em."

Betty didn't look at Jesse, but she was listening.

"Then she came home to Highlands County, and she knew she had come to a good place, but she had to get strong before she could be with others of her own kind."

Jess stopped and was quiet for so long that Betty thought he was through, but just as she started to turn and take the first step away from the pen, Jess added, "I figgered she'd let go and fly, someday. We just had to wait till everything was right."

"You think everything is all right, now?" she asked, and turned to look at Jess's thin, wrinkled face.

"Well," he said, gazing intently at the chickens. Seconds slid away, a minute, and finally he raised his face to hers. The crows' feet deepened. "I reckon so."

Betty felt her own face matching his, smile for smile. "Maybe so," she said. "Why don't you stay and have supper with me? We could have new lettuce and onions."

"I reckon I could handle that," he answered, and they walked together across the yard towards Betty's homeplace. Tildy moved among the young hens Jesse had brought, a big, white soft-looking bird with toughness underneath and a glint in her golden eye.

Ralphie

The thing about Ralph, Mary thought, was that he just never stopped growing. He weighed ten pounds, two ounces at birth, and even though the doctor told her it was normal for babies to lose a little weight between the time when they went home from the hospital and when they came back for the one-week checkup, Ralphie didn't. He didn't lose an ounce then, and he had never lost an ounce since.

Everyone used to say he was a beautiful baby, and he was, never fat but always robust. There were lines around his wrists and ankles like someone had tied a string and pulled it tight. There were dimples on his knuckles and knees,and his baby feet were nearly as thick as they were long.

"Are you feeding this baby table food?" asked the pediatrician, at Ralphie's three-month examination.

"No, nothing but breast milk. Not even water. Just like you said," Mary replied. And the doctor nodded, and patted the baby's thigh - which a lot of people did. It seemed as though Ralphie's legs were impossible to resist, in those days. The doctor said he was a fine, healthy baby, and to stick with just breast milk for three more months.

Mary did, and went on nursing Ralphie for eleven more months after that, supplementing with mashed vegetables and Cheerios until Ralphie was fourteen months old. Breastfeeding such a big child scandalized her husband's mother, and even Mary's own mother hinted that eight or ten months would have been enough, but Mary's grandmother told her that when the baby was ready to be weaned he would let Mary know, and that she should not listen to middle-aged women who were trying to get above their raising.

So Mary continued to offer her breast to Ralphie when he went down for a nap or for the night, and sure enough, at fourteen months he just lost interest. Mary's milk dried up without the first bit of trouble, and Ralphie was the sweetest-tempered baby there ever was. He slept through the night at six weeks, and continued to do so every night of his life after that, as far as Mary knew. He was never sick, never had his first cold till he was five years old and started school. And he was never picky, but always ate whatever the rest of the family had.

And he grew and grew. When Ralphie went for his last checkup with the pediatrician, when he was 17 and getting ready for his senior year of football, the doctor showed Ralphie's growth chart to Mary. She looked at the pages of graphs, with the National Center for Health Statistics percentiles for length and weight (birth to 36 months) and height and weight (2 to 18 years) printed on them, and at the long series of dots and connecting lines that delineated her son's life. There, marked in ink, was verification of Ralphie's development. Just as Mary had suspected, it clearly showed that her son was above the rest. It was like another lifeline, marked on the chart in the doctor's firm, precise handwriting. Ralphie's line arced gracefully, roughly paralleling but always sailing above the lines for 50 percentile, 75 percentile, even 95 percentile.

"It's good the way Ralphie's height has kept pace with his weight," the doctor said. "Still, after football season, he might want to try to knock off a few pounds. Do you think the team will have a good season this year?"

"Yeah, I think so." Ralphie smiled at Doc Thompson, who had seen him through the bumps and bruises he'd sustained as a pony league, little league, junior high and senior high starting linebacker.

"Good, good," Doc said, and tapped Ralphie's knee with the closed folder holding Ralphie's records. People still had a tendency to touch Ralphie, to pat his back or rub his head. "You just keep knockin' 'em flat, Ralphie."

"I'll try," Ralphie replied, and Mary thought that was a perfect summation of Ralphie's attitude: I'll try. And when he tried, he did well. He did so well at school that he was inducted into the Beta Club during his junior year of high school, and during his senior year he won a place on the all-regional football team, voted on by the area's newspaper sportswriters and pictured in the paper.

Everybody liked Ralphie. He was popular with the boys on the teams, and teachers wrote things like "Ralph is such a nice young man. He's a pleasure to have in my classroom!" on his report cards. Girls called him on the telephone, to cry about their boyfriends or ask for advice on how to attract some other boy's notice. Ralphie was always sympathetic, and encouraging, and helpful.

During the summers, when he helped on the farm, the older men played jokes on Ralphie, and thumped him on the back when he fell for the gags. Ralphie always laughed along with them, and took the joking in stride. He seemed to understand it was the only way those men knew to express their tenderness for such a big, gentle boy.

Mary was a little shocked to realize how many years had passed since Ralphie was born, when he ordered a class ring and graduation announcements. She could easily pick him out of the long double line of capped and gowned seniors marching slowly down the aisle of the auditorium. Seventeen years old he was, and head and shoulders above the rest. No other student even came close. He was awarded several athletic prizes and a large scholarship to a small college 150 miles away.

"College" was a name and place of mystery to Mary. Neither she nor her husband nor any of her immediate family had ever set foot on a college campus. In all of Mary's extended family network of cousins, nieces, uncles and kin-by-marriage, only the daughter of one of Mary's nieces had gone to college. According to the girl's grandmother, the child had been lost to the family after only one year at school. After the first semester she'd seemed glad to be home for the Christmas break, but by the end of the first year, things were different. She'd taken up smoking cigarettes, and during that summer she made numerous long-distance telephone calls to her college friends, pulling the long cord of the kitchen telephone so she could sit on the back steps and talk and smoke, and knock cigarette ashes on the roots of the lilac bush. The next year she hadn't come home at all, but had stayed at college to take some kind of summer job.

After that, the girl was simply gone, as cut out of the life of the family as if she'd had an identity change - like the sex changes some of Oprah's guests talked about having, that made them into who they "really" were. She'd graduated and taken a job in a city out west. One day she'd called her parents to tell them she'd gotten married, and then, three years later, called to tell them she'd gotten a divorce. In between she'd come home for once-a-year visits, but no one knew her any more, and the visits were a strain.

Of course, such a thing couldn't happen to Ralphie. Ralphie was a good boy. It was true he was a good student, more than bright enough to get along. But Mary had been very careful not to let Ralphie get the idea that he was better than anyone else, or special in any way. It had been rumored among the family that the other poor girl was a little too smart, petted and made over by her teachers. She had been told repeatedly that she was special, which had made her dissatisfied. The only thing Mary ever told Ralphie was special about him was that he was an especially nice boy. She hadn't thought there could be any harm in that.

The night of Ralphie's graduation, Mary sat up late and watched television by herself. The local station showed a re-run of an old variety show featuring a skit by Emmett Kelly, the Ringling Brothers Circus clown. The announcer talked about the "comedic genius" of Emmett Kelly, so Mary waited specially to see the clown do his act. She hadn't been to a circus since Ralphie was little.

She was surprised by the clown's frown and quiet demeanor. She waited for the joke, for the bucket of water that suddenly turned into confetti, or for the slip and fall that would have the audience guffawing. Instead the hobo clown silently gazed into the eyes of the people in the audience, then began to sweep a medallion of light on the canvas floor into a smaller and smaller circle. The darkness at the back of the crowd of happy families closed around him. Finally the clown swept the tiny spot of light on the canvas floor completely out and the audience responded with a rich wave of applause and whistling that rolled out of the darkness. But Mary hadn't seen anything funny. Instead, Mary began to cry. She quickly wiped her face with her hands and blew her nose into a pale pink Kleenex, and briefly wondered why this sad-faced clown was famous.

In September Ralphie went away to college, sitting beside his father in the old sedan. Mary waved good-bye and then watched from behind the screen door as they moved slowly down the graveled road, pulling behind them a puffy tail of dust, dull and furry in the directionless light before the sun climbed over the ridge. The car turned onto the paved road, and Mary lost track of them. She knew they would travel the twelve curvy miles to town and there climb the entrance ramp onto the interstate; then they'd head into the rising sun as they drove toward college. It would take three hours to drive to college, and three hours for her husband to return.

Christmas drew near and Mary waited for Ralphie to come home. He called to tell them he had arranged a ride, and Mary thought how like Ralphie it was to keep his father from making the long, tiring trip to college and back in one day.

Mary shopped for her son's Christmas gifts, buying white cotton jockey shorts and T-shirts, dark-colored socks and a nice flannel shirt, just as she had every year since Ralphie was out of diapers. She hesitated over his "fun" gift, his "Santa Claus," as she still thought of it, though Ralphie had stopped believing in Santa a long time ago. Ralphie had had a birthday since he'd gone away to college, and he was eighteen, now. What did boys of eighteen do for fun? she wondered. No "boy of eighteen" had ever lived in her house, eaten at her table, left dirty clothing in the bathroom hamper for her to wash, had done any of the things through which Mary could have deciphered the riddle of his personality.

She stood in the aisle of the J C Penny store, frozen by a sudden fear of opening her home to an unknown, perhaps fierce, young man. But then, after being nudged by a large woman in an out-of-date, fur-collared coat whose red-cheeked, country face was wrapped around an unsophisticated grin, ("'Scuse me, and Merry Christmas, dear!" the woman said.) Mary corrected herself. This wasn't some stranger coming to her house for Christmas dinner, this was Ralphie, her son, the same boy who'd eaten every Christmas dinner of his sweet young life at her table. Finally, on the advice of a sales clerk, Mary bought a boxed set of toiletries for Ralphie: soap-on-a-rope, aftershave, a short-handled hair brush, and a wide deodorant, all, except the brush, scented alike. "Every guy at Tech needs one of these," the clerk said, and Mary hadn't bothered to say that her son didn't go to Tech and was a nice young man, not a "guy."

For Ralphie's homecoming, Mary cooked. She'd already prepared all of Ralphie's favorite cookies, plus fudge and peanut butter balls and candied pecans and even the confectioner's sugar and peanut butter roll-ups that were not strictly a Christmas candy, but which had been a favorite of Ralphie's since he was a toddler. For his homecoming supper she planned to serve fried chicken, gravy, mashed potatoes, slaw, green beans canned out of her garden, and corn on the cob, picked while August heat beat down on her shoulders and ran off her face as sweat. Mary almost always cut corn off the cob, to save freezer space, but this year she had put aside a few perfect ears to have when Ralphie came home. And she planned to bake Ralphie's favorite apple pie too, despite the panty shelf already groaning under the weight of her holiday baking.

Throughout the day, as she worked, Mary left her kitchen to look out the front window. The corn field marched away from the edge of the driveway, its decimated stalks reduced to ranked stobs. An undecided gray sky, neither cloudy nor bright, clenched itself to the tops of the ridges, and a raven sliced his way across it, his rusty croak keeping time, Mary knew, with the flapping of his wings. She had heard the raven's calls throughout the summer and fall, and easily recognized them and his rough-edged silhouette. They grated on her nerves. Her husband had told her the raven had a nest on the cliffs lining the bend of river that thrust into their land, and had started to tell her about the raven's intelligence and funny tricks. But Mary didn't want to understand this or any other bird's habits or reasons. She only knew it had broken into her peace and calm, whether she was weeding or harvesting in her garden or working in her flowers, and now here it was again, cutting the sky into boundaries with his dark wings. She had a swift, savage wish that the raven would die and leave her skies smooth and solid, and then, frightened by the momentary passion, Mary went back to her kitchen.

Ralphie finally came. Mary was looking out the window when a strange car stopped at the end of the graveled road. Someone got out of the back seat, walked to the rear of the car, opened the trunk. Mary wasn't sure who it was until the person had lifted a bag from the trunk, slammed the lid shut, and waved to the car's passengers as they sped away on the hardtop road. Then she recognized his movements, the set of his head above his shoulders.

She watched for a few seconds, then turned away and hurried into the kitchen. She stirred the beans, took the chicken out of the skillet, added flour to the drippings for gravy. Then she went back to the window and looked out at her son.

Ralphie was wearing the letter jacket he'd earned twice over, playing football. He trudged up the road in the steady, heavy walk Mary knew, and stepped onto the driveway without looking up.

While he was crossing the yard, using his old shortcut from driveway's edge to front step, he stopped and turned up his face. It was after five o'clock and the winter daylight was nearly gone, but he stopped in the shaft of light thrown out from the window, and Mary could see that Ralphie's eyes were closed, that he held his bare face exposed to whatever hovered over the farm.

Mary strode to the front door, grabbed the knob, jerked the door open. "Ralphie?" she said. "Ralphie, why don't you come on in the house?"

"Hi, Mom," he said. "It's starting to snow."

"Yes, I see. Supper's just about ready. Come in and eat."

"Okay, Mom. Coming." After glancing again into the beam of light - or the darkness behind it - he came in.

Mary thought the holiday went well, with Ralphie falling quickly into their old patterns and habits. The only thing different was that Ralphie, raised with a farmer's habit of rising early, now wanted to sleep late. Even on Christmas morning, Mary had to call her son, to tell him to get up and have Christmas, so they could eat breakfast and get things ready for the relatives who were coming for Christmas dinner.

On New Year's Eve, Ralphie called the friend with whom he'd ridden home, and arranged the time and place to meet for the return trip. After he left, Mary carefully told her family that Ralphie seemed to like college, seemed to be getting along with his classmates and classes, seemed glad to get home for the holidays, had seemed neither glad nor sad to go back. She settled into the dark, sleepy rhythms of winter. She cleaned her house once a week, went to town for groceries every other Friday, and went to church on Sundays when the weather wasn't too bad. In February she ordered garden seed from the company she'd used every year since her marriage, and thought that if the raven croaked his curses at her this year, she'd ask Ralphie to shoot it.

In spring Ralphie came home, and Mary thought he seemed thinner. "Have you lost weight, son?" she asked, and felt a small flicker, just a wing-brush, of uneasiness.

"No, Mom, I weigh exactly the same," he said.

"Oh, good," Mary replied. "I don't want you getting all thin and weak from studying too much."

"No, I'm not studying too much," he said, keeping his eyes on the horizon. "Did Dad go to town to get the fertilizer?"

"Yes." Mary wondered what her son was looking for. "Why don't you come in and rest until he gets back?"

"Mom." Ralphie turned and looked at her. "I'm not tired, I'm not losing weight. I am an inch taller. I'm just growing up, that's all. I think I'll walk down to the river, I haven't been down there in a long time."

Mary didn't reply, but watched her son cross the front yard and start through the plowed corn field. He walked quickly, swinging his arms and stepping from one turned furrow to the second one away, taking long, even strides. He did seem taller, and Mary frowned. Was it normal for a child to continue to grow after he turned eighteen? Shouldn't all Ralphie's growing be done now, finished while he was living under her roof, eating her good food, wearing the clothing she adjusted to his size?

"Watch out for that raven!" she called, and Ralphie lifted one hand to show he'd heard, but Mary wasn't sure he'd understood.

When September came and Ralphie went back to school, Mary stood again on her porch and waved. She sighed and when the thought came to her that she wasn't sure whether it was a sigh of regret at Ralphie's leaving or a small, a very small, sigh of relief, Mary jerked her head and walked back to the kitchen with loud steps. Why would she be relieved that her son, her sweet boy, was going so far away, to be gone for months, to be under the influence of people she didn't know? What a strange notion. Maybe she was starting to go through the change, women do get odd ideas at that time, she thought.

Ralphie's second year of college passed as quietly as the first, but when he came home for the summer, Mary knew to a certainty that he was thinner.

"You have lost weight," she accused. "These are not the jeans we sent you for your birthday. I've never seen this brand of jeans before, and look here, they're thirty-sixes, not thirty-eights like you've worn for three years!" Mary stood in the doorway of Ralphie's room, holding the jeans before her, turned partly inside out with the yellow and blue evidence of the tag, sewn into the inside of the zipper, thrust forward.

Ralphie was sitting on the edge of his bed, and he looked up from the paperback book he'd been reading, frowning at Mary as though puzzled by who she was or why she should be holding his dirty clothes.

"Mom, you don't have to do my laundry. I do it at school all the time, I can take care of it myself."

Mary stood holding the strange pants, which seemed of their own volition to sink toward the floor. "But they're the wrong size," she said.

"No, that's my size now. Look, they're longer than the ones I used to wear, too. Thirty-fours. I just keep growing, Mom."

"I think you should go see Doctor Thompson," she said, faintly.

"Doc Thompson? Mom, he's a pediatrician. I'm nineteen years old now, he wouldn't see me even if I was sick."

"But he knows you, he's been your doctor since you were born. He knows your history, has your charts and everything. He'd be worried because you're losing weight."

"No he wouldn't. I'm not sick, Mom, I'm fine. I don't need a doctor, and I don't need you to fuss over me. Okay?"

Mary didn't feel that things were "okay," but she didn't feel strong enough to stand there and straighten them out. She felt weak, and tired, and worn. She hadn't done any more work this morning than usual, but she had the sudden thought that it would be nice to sit down in her husband's recliner and push the handle so the footrest would come up. "Well," she said as she turned away, "I guess we can talk it over with Daddy."

"Mom," he said, as she started up the hall. Ralphie rose from the bed and walked to her side. "Give me these. I'll take care of my laundry." He gently pulled the jeans from her hands, smiled at her, then turned to go back into his room. He dropped the dirty jeans in the floor, scooped up the paperback, and laid down on top of the quilted bedspread Mary had made when Ralphie was twelve.

Still lots of good in that spread, she thought.

That evening, when Mary was bringing a plate of biscuits to the supper table and arranging words to say to her husband so he would make Ralphie go for a checkup, she found that Ralphie had already started a conversation with his father.

"If you'd let me use the car, I could work for them four days a week, and help you two days."

Mary set the biscuits down, turned and walked back into the kitchen. She looked at the top of the electric stove, but there were no dishes of food waiting to be carried to the table. She turned in a complete circle, trying to remember why she'd come back to the kitchen, but she couldn't think. In a small corner of her heart she wondered who, who would Ralphie work for, four days a week? but her mind had no answer for that, either, and her feet seemed unwilling to take her back to where Ralphie and his father were talking and making decisions. Finally she got a stick of margarine out of the refrigerator and walked with it, still in its foil wrapper, back to the table.

"...good money," Ralphie was saying. "I'll be working at

school, too, so maybe by next summer I can buy my own car." He took a biscuit from the plate and handed it to his father.

The older man spoke slowly as he broke open the bread and reached for the bowl of gravy. Mary always set the gravy at her husband's left hand. "I'll ask around, keep an eye out. Maybe a good used car will come available."

Mary sat down at her place. "Why would you need a car? You can use your daddy's whenever you need to."

"Upperclassmen can keep a car on campus," Ralphie said. He was spooning squash cooked with onions onto his plate. Mary thought that he didn't seem to eat much biscuit and gravy any more. "Maybe next year, a couple of guys and I may find an apartment and live off campus. It's a lot cheaper. I'd definitely need a car then."

Silence fell over the table, folding around the three people and their brief motions as they put Mary's food into their mouths.

Ralphie went to work with a masonry crew that was erecting brick chimneys and fireplaces in a new apartment complex in town. Mondays through Thursdays he rose at 4:30, and was dressed (in his shabbiest jeans and T-shirts) and out the door by 5 AM. All day he mixed mortar with sand and water, shoveled the wet mud into wheelbarrows, and pushed load after load of it to the masons. Or he threw bricks, one at a time, to the masons who were working from scaffolding.

The crew worked until six o'clock or later, hurrying to get this project done while their summer helpers were out of school and before bad weather came.

Each evening Ralphie drove their old Plymouth slowly home, slowly came into the house, and went straight into the shower, where he stood in the hot water for longer than Mary thought was necessary. At first Mary got up at 4:00 and cooked breakfast for Ralphie, but Ralphie told her that he really didn't have time to sit down and eat. She packed lunches for him until he told her it was just as easy for him to eat what the rest of the crew had - fast food from the nearest convenience store. She tried to repair the splits in the knees of his pants until he told her to forget it. "The bricks just eat them up," he said.

On Fridays and Saturdays Ralphie worked in the fields with his father and the neighbors with whom they shared labor. On Sundays he slept late and sometimes went out with friends for a while after supper. But he always came home early and went to bed, ready to start the next week of work.

Mary saw her cousin in the grocery store. They assured each other they were well, exchanged comments about the weather. "We went out to look at those new apartments E & L is building," the cousin said.

Mary thought it was just like this woman to indulge in idle curiosity.

"I saw your Ralphie out there working in the sun. He sure is getting tan, isn't he?"

Mary murmured agreement, though she hadn't particularly noticed.

"You certainly did a good job of raising that boy," the woman ran on. "A lot of boys, they get out into the world a little bit and they just keep going. Not many of them will come back home and work like that. Not many kids will get a college education and be satisfied back home on the farm."

Mary said she couldn't take the credit, that Ralphie had always been a good boy, and said she'd better get on home, there were beans waiting to be picked.

When she got home and was bending into the back seat of the car, lifting the paper bags - which she'd had to request specially, because she hated the thin plastic bags - of groceries into her arms, Mary heard the raven squawking overhead. She straightened and quickly turned so her back was against the side of the car, and squinted to spot the raven's silhouette against the bright sky. She saw him clearly, and heard again his rough cry. It made her jaw teeth ache. A taste came into Mary's mouth like the first faint souring of leftover beans, that soon would be stinking and foul. She wanted to drop the groceries and press her hands over her ears, but she didn't. She carried the groceries into her house and got on about the business of the day.

At three-thirty that afternoon, Mary lifted the last canner of green beans off the stove. The weight on top of the pressure vent had been hissing and jiggling for twenty-five minutes, filling the house with angry steam, and the sudden silence of its finishing seemed to race outward from the canner, hurting Mary's ears with a shock wave even more fierce than the hissing had been. She was standing with her hands on the canner handles, letting the soft bumping and settling of the jars inside soothe away the memory of the pressure, when she heard a car coming up the graveled driveway.

Mary went to the living room window and looked out, and recognized their Plymouth. She opened the door, went out, walked to the car as Ralphie was emerging from the opposite side.

"Ralphie, what is it? You're home so early." Then she saw the cut on one cheekbone, the swelling at the corner of his mouth and around the opposite eye. There was a hint of crusty blood around one nostril. "Was there an accident?" she asked, frightened. "Did you fall?"

"Nah, I didn't fall." Ralphie seemed relaxed and calm, and even a little jovial.

"But you're hurt," Mary said. She looked at his face more closely, saw that bruises were beginning to form under the skin. "You're hurt."

"Mom, I'm okay. I just had a little disagreement with a couple of the guys at work. I'm fine. I'm going to go shower."

He patted her on the shoulder as he walked past her, but Mary turned and caught his arm near the elbow, and held him back. "A disagreement? But what happened to your face? How were you hurt? Did you go to the doctor?"

"Lord, Mom, I don't need to see the doctor. It was just a little fight, I've been banged up worse playing football. Let me get cleaned up."

"Fight? What do you mean, 'fight'? Do you mean someone hit you? Did some man hit you, Ralphie?"

He turned to face her fully, and looked down at her with his face beginning to be distorted by the results of his "disagreement."

"Yes, a man hit me. And I hit him. I gave as good as I got, or better.

"But... But Ralphie, we don't fight, in this family. I've told you never to hit anybody. I've told you! Oh, what happened, to make you hit somebody?"

Ralphie looked and looked at Mary, until she wanted to scream at him, or to run into the house and close the door against him, but she clenched her teeth and held to his arm until he said, "I told them I wouldn't be called 'Fat Boy' anymore, Mom. I just told them, and made sure they understood I meant it."

"What? You got into a fight over name calling? Oh Ralphie, how could you? You'll have to apologize, and -"

With a movement that was only a rapid blur at the corner of her vision, he lifted her hand from his arm, and she fell as abruptly silent as if he'd covered her mouth. They stood so close together that she could smell sweat and the dust of concrete and even the musky hint of blood on him, and the cigarettes the other men smoked at break times. But he kept her hand in his, tethering her, creating an umbilical between them. She thought that if she let down her guard, if she opened the floodgates through which she had poured life into him while he was still unborn and hidden in her body, that a reversal would occur and his huge and overwhelmingly masculine energy would pour into her.

It would drown her. It would kill her. She would be extinguished, like a pale flame washed over by water. She wanted to free her hand, but he held her firmly.

"Mom. Don't be silly. I'm not in kindergarten, this wasn't name-calling. It was harassment, and I don't have to subject myself to it. I shouldn't have kept quiet as long as I did. Now the men know who I am."

Mary jerked her hand away from him. "Well, I don't! I don't know who you are, you're not my Ralphie any more, not my son, not my baby who was so beautiful and sweet. That school changed you. You went there and got thinner, and your clothes don't fit, and I don't know who you are!" The words came spewing out of Mary's mouth; they made a hissing in her ears. She gasped, so horrified by what she had heard that she pressed both hands against her lips, weighing them down, shutting the angry pressure inside her mouth and down her throat, where she was choking.

High above and far away, the raven called.

Mary shrieked. "I hate that thing! I hate it, I hate it, it torments me!" She ran to the door and threw it open. Inside, she raced into the bedroom she'd shared with her husband for twenty-two years, and pulled his old shotgun off the gun rack. She ran back through the living room and onto the front porch.

Ralph was standing in the yard, his head tilted, looking up. When she ran, struggling for breath, onto the grass and he saw what she carried, he asked, "Mom?"

Mary heaved the old gun to her shoulder, and held the end of the barrel up. She pivoted on her left heel, her teeth clenched, her eyes raking the sky.

"Mom," Ralph said.

Finally she saw him, saw the clownish bird who hadn't made her laugh, the raucous bird who'd shattered her cultivated quiet, the black scheming bird who'd taken his territory from hers and mated and raised young in it. She closed her eyes and screamed and squeezed the triggers of the shotgun, one and then the second, as quickly as she could get her finger on it.

The shotgun shoved Mary's shoulder so that she staggered. She kept the gun stock in her arms, its butt pressed against her shoulder, but the barrel was pulled toward the ground like a magnet drawn to true north. She might have been taking aim at a mole, except that her eyes were still closed.

In a few moments, she felt Ralphie come near. She turned her blind face away from his presence.

"Let me carry this for you," he said. The shotgun was lifted from her hands.

Her eyes were closed, her face averted. "Did I kill it?"

"No."

No. He was too far away from her, flying too high.

"Let's go in." He led her up the step onto the porch, through the door, into the living room. "Do you want to lay down?"

"No. Let me sit. Let me sit in your father's chair."

He led her to the recliner, eased her sinking into it, pushed the lever to raise the footrest. She pressed her cheek against the soft fabric covering the chair, her eyes still closed. She felt him go away, and then come back. "Do you want a blanket?" he asked.

"No. I'll get up in a minute."

He hesitated, then said, "I'm going to get cleaned up now. If you need me for anything, knock on the bathroom door. I might not hear you if you just call."

"I'm fine." Sitting in the darkness of her closed eyes, she raised her head a little from the chair, tilted it in the direction of his voice. "Did I hurt that bird at all?"

"Nah. I don't think you even came close."

Mary lay in the red darkness behind her closed eyes. She heard drawers open and close in Ralphie's room, heard the bathroom door shut and the soft snap of its lock being turned. The hot water handle in the shower squeaked its accustomed two-toned complaint, then water drummed steadily against the shower stall floor. In the warm familiarity of sound, Mary began to put the morning's events out of her mind. She pushed the memory of her actions into a part of her mind where it seemed that warm threads of water were pouring down, where the powerful, dark thoughts would be bathed and rinsed, where the cold hard feel of the shotgun in her hands would be softened and eventually drained away in a sinking swirl.

In the bathroom, Ralphie began to sing.

Touched

"Isn't it too bad about Mary Lou Powers?" Aunt Judy said. Aunt Judy is my mother's younger sister. "Imagine getting run over by a train right there in town."

I was eight years old that spring evening when I was made to sit with the women in Aunt Nellie's living room. I would rather have stayed with the men and boys on the back porch, and listened to them talking about whose hounds were running good, but Mom had given me that certain look, and I knew I had to come in.

Aunt Nellie was actually my great-aunt, my dead grandmother's sister, and even though we used the less formal title, she was not a casual person. At Aunt Nellie's we were not allowed to run in the house, and if we came inside we had to sit quietly and not speak until spoken to.

I stopped swinging my feet and straightened my spine. Tragic accidents were not discussed in front of the children in my family, and I was fascinated by them. I sat taller so I wouldn't miss a single word, and wondered why it was worse to be run over by a train in town.

"Well, was she in the family way, or not?" Aunt Eva, Mom's

older sister, asked. "I've heard both ways."

"She'd only been married three weeks," Mom said.

Aunt Eva replied, "That don't mean a thing."

"You know," Aunt Nellie said, and sighed. "I knew that girl was not long for this world. I had a vision."

Mom and Aunt Judy didn't respond, and I could tell by the way Aunt Judy rubbed her fingers together that she was wishing for a cigarette. Smoking was not allowed in Aunt Nellie's house, especially by women.

"A vision?" Aunt Eva asked. She had eaten all her gingersnaps and was holding her little china plate aloft in her left hand, her elbow propped on the ruffled doily spread like a petrified spiderweb on the table beside her chair.

"I was walking home from Mable Snider's Tupperware party, about a week before the wedding," Aunt Nellie said. She gazed across the room, her eyes focused on things not of this world. "Your Uncle Raymond had offered to come pick me up in the car, but it's not but a quarter of a mile and there were so many cars parked at Mable's that I knew he'd have trouble turning the Lincoln around."

Aunt Nellie always referred to their car by its model name. Daddy said that was so everybody would know they weren't still driving the horsecart Uncle Raymond had married her in.

"It was a nice night, very warm and clear. I looked up into the sky to give my thanks to God for all His wonderful blessings and to ask Him to keep Ocie Burcham's boar hog inside his fence till I got in the house, and there it was, clear as a bell."

"The hog?" Aunt Eva whispered.

"A vision, right there before my eyes."

"What kind of a vision?" Aunt Eva unpropped her elbow and leaned forward.

"Eva, for goodness' sake," Mom whispered.

"As soon as I saw it, I knew what it meant," Aunt Nellie went on. "There it was, spread across half the sky, plain for those who would read it."

"What did it say?" Aunt Eva was getting impatient.

"There was a picture of a brides' veil, then a big plus sign, then a picture of the front of a car, then a equals sign, and then a grave-stone, and on the gravestone, the letters R, I, P."

"R, I, P?" Aunt Eva said. "Mary Lou's initials were M, L, T; not R, I, P. Do we know anybody whose initials are R, I, P?"

Aunt Judy snorted. "Rest In Peace, Eva, Rest In Peace!"

"I knew the message was for Mary Lou, because at the party we had just been discussing the wedding. Several of the women were ordering Tupperware for wedding gifts." Aunt Nellie sniffed and came back from wherever she'd been looking.

"Did you go back to Mable's and get the other ladies to look at this vision?" Mom asked

"I did not," Aunt Nellie answered. "I came right on home and went to bed."

"Didn't you even get Uncle Raymond to look at it?"

"Your Uncle Raymond hasn't been awake after eight-thirty in twenty-two years. I wasn't about to disturb him for what was clearly meant to be a message to me. I was there to see it. I was praying to God. He wanted to let me know about this event, and He did. Would anyone like more coffee?" That was the signal for everyone to stand up, brush her skirt, carry the little china plates to the kitchen. The men and boys were rounded up and we sorted ourselves into the right cars and left Aunt Nellie's.

On the ride home, Mom told Daddy that Aunt Nellie claimed she'd had a vision.

Daddy wanted to know what kind of a vision Aunt Nellie had, and Mom told him about it.

Daddy said that it sounded to him like Mable Snider had put too much gin in the punch, and played one too many party games. Mom said "Jimmy Neal," which was Daddy's name, in a shocked voice, but she laughed.

But I believed that Aunt Nellie had seen a vision of God's In-tent, and I wanted to see one too. I thought it would be the neatest, scariest thing ever. I began to look for God's hand everywhere.

That summer I prayed a lot. I recited "Now I lay me down to sleep" every night when I got into bed, and I prayed before every meal, too, though I had to do it in my head, silently. The first time I asked a blessing, my older brother stopped chewing, stared at me over the gravy and mashed potatoes, and said, "What're you doing?"

I felt my cheeks heating up, but I said, "Praying."

"What for?" he asked. Asking a blessing for food was something our family could do when the occasion demanded, but it was nothing we did regularly. Mom's fried chicken was good eating, but it hadn't made anybody else pray.

"I just want to," I mumbled.

"Hey Mom!" Billy yelled, "Darlene's praying."

My little brother Jim looked up from stirring the food on his plate. "Darlene's praying?" he asked in a hopeful tone.

"Shut up," I hissed. I knew he was hoping for a distraction from eating, any distraction. Daddy thought Jim was wormy. Every few weeks he gave Jim a dose of worm medicine. We all had to take it once a year, but Jim got it more often because he was skinny and didn't eat a lot. Anything that took attention off his plate was welcome to Jim.

"What're you praying for, Darlene?" Mom asked in a mild tone, as she set the biscuits on the table. "Jimmy Neal, would you like a glass of milk before I sit down?"

Daddy said yes and I thought I'd escaped, but Billy said loudly, "Yeah, what're you praying for, are you praying that Tim Blevins will sit with you on the bus tomorrow?"

"No, I am not! I hate Tim Blevins!" In fact, I had a crush on Tim Blevins, and wished he would sit with me on the bus, but I would've died under torture before admitting it.

"No yelling at the table," Mom said, as she set a glass of milk beside Daddy's plate. Jim had begun reciting "Tim and Darlene, setting in a tree, k-i-s-s-i-n-g," so I kicked him under the table, and he howled, and Daddy said,

"Here now, you kids!"

And that was the end of that.

From then on I asked a blessing with my eyes open and my mouth shut, but it didn't feel like it was doing as much good as the other way. I tried to make up for it by praying for Billy to get called by God to be a missionary in Africa, since I didn't figure I should pray for him to die outright. Once he got over there, the headhunters could take care of him and I wouldn't have to put up with him any more, and meanwhile I was getting in more praying than I ever had before.

After a week I still hadn't had a vision, and I decided I would have to be good, too. As far as I could tell, Aunt Nellie behaved all the time. She surely never had to be reminded to keep her feet off the furniture, since she was too round and old to raise them up that high. She didn't have to brush her teeth every night, since I'd personally seen hers soaking in a glass of water in the bathroom, when she stayed with us while Uncle Raymond had a hernia operation. And if she thought those gingersnap cookies were a treat fit for company, there was nothing anyone could put on her plate that she wouldn't finish up with ease.

Near the end of summer, during the heat of dog days, Aunt Nellie called my mother to say that she had five bushels of tomatoes picked, and if Mom would come over and help can them, she could have half the finished product. I knew for a fact there were plenty of tomatoes in our own garden, but Mom said it was our duty to help Aunt Nellie, so she loaded extra canning jars, screw-on rings and flat lids, the water-bath canning kettle, and my brothers and me into the car and drove to Aunt Nellie's house. On the way she gave us a (small) list of things we could do, and another (much longer) list of things we were absolutely not allowed to do.

"Billy, it would be best if you and Jim just stay out of the house. You know how Aunt Nellie is about dirt getting tracked in on her carpet. Darlene, you can help us in the kitchen if you want to, or you can stay with the boys, but you all have to keep out of trouble. Don't go off the farm, and don't get in the corn field and break down the stalks. You can wade in the creek, but don't get your clothes wet, and don't come trying to scare us with the biggest crawdad you find. Don't come begging for drinks every whipstitch. I brought a thermos of Kool Aid, you can set it on the edge of the porch and get a drink when you need it, but try not to spill it on the porch. It'll draw wasps."

"Yes ma'am," Billy said.

"Please stay out of trouble, kids. I want to get this done and us back home in time to fix a decent supper."

"Yes, Mom," we all mumbled.

I made up my mind to help in the kitchen, because that would constitute "being good," and I could hear any interesting talk that took place over the tomatoes. Also I could watch Aunt Nellie in action. I wanted to see if she prayed out loud over the canner.

It was hot in Aunt Nellie's kitchen. She had a pan of water steaming on the stove when we went in, and a pan of ice water on the counter nearby. There were bushels of smooth red tomatoes lined up by the back door. Aunt Nellie had a system for working up tomatoes: wash, scald, dip in ice water, peel, cut chunks into the waiting quart jars. I was assigned the job of dropping clean tomatoes into the steaming water and then quickly using a big slotted spoon to lift them out and slide them into the ice water. I stood on an old kitchen chair so I could see into the pans, and my head was in a cloud of sharp-smelling steam. I could see the thin tomato skins splitting and curling in long curving furrows an instant after I put them in the cold water, and soon I thought the skin on my face would do that too, if I could stick it in the cold water with the tomatoes.

It wasn't long before Mom and Aunt Nellie had a canner of filled quart jars on the back of the stove. The water surrounding the jars had to come to a boil before we started counting down the minutes for processing, and the kettle on the back of the stove added to the heat and humidity.

Standing over the kettles of tomatoes and the steaming pans was like hanging my head over the lip of a volcano. Aunt Nellie and Mom talked, but only about gardens and the price of groceries and how many sweet potatoes they expected to have this year.

A second canner of tomatoes was added to the stove top, and the heat turned on beneath it.

I dipped tomatoes in the simmering water, and lifted them out. I dropped tomatoes in ice water, and lifted them out. Tomatoes in, tomatoes out, tomatoes in, tomatoes out. Little trickles of condensed tomato steam ran down my neck, and the front of my T-shirt stuck to my chest.

The chair wobbled under my feet, and then Mom was beside me, saying "Get down off that chair, Darlene, before you fall down."

She wiped my face with her apron and said, "I think you've helped enough. Why don't you go on outside, get a drink of Kool

Aid, and play with your brothers for a while? Go find some place cool."

I went out the back door and staggered to the vicinity of the thermos. When I pressed the little lever on the bottom of the jug, green Kool Aid trickled into a paper cup. I gulped it down, refilled the cup, and sat for a few minutes, sipping and squinting into the bright sunlight in Aunt Nellie's back yard. Billy's and Jim's heads bobbed up from behind the hill above the creek, and I watched as they strolled along the cornfield fence, Billy leading, Jim dragging the toes of his tennis shoes in the dry grass. They stopped walking and stood by the fence. I drained the cup of Kool Aid, gulped one more for good measure, and walked through the steely sun to join them by the fence.

"It's hot in there," I said.

"It's hot out here," Billy replied, but he gazed intently among the tall stalks of corn. "Guess what?" he added.

"What?"

"Mr. Burcham's pigs have got into Uncle Raymond's corn."

I looked at the rows of tall field corn, but I couldn't see any evidence of pigs. I drained the Kool Aid from the cup in my hand. The sun was straight up in the sky, and I felt it pushing down on my head with a hot, heavy hand.

Billy started climbing the woven-wire fence.

"Hey!" yelled Jim. "What're you doing?"

"Mr. Burcham's pigs are not supposed to be in Uncle Raymond's corn," Billy said as he worked his way up carefully, staying close to the fence post. "Let's go chase 'em out."

"Mom told us not to go in there," I mumbled. Somehow, I didn't feel like talking.

"She told us not to break down the corn stalks. Well, I ain't about to break down any corn. We'll go between the rows, it's like roads in there. Besides, you know they'd want us to get the pigs out."

"I'm gonna tell Momma!" Jim wailed. He was only five, and he was afraid of getting whipped and afraid of pigs and probably afraid of going in among the endless stalks of tall, rustly corn. It felt like being on the edge of a jungle, just standing at the edge of the corn field.

Billy crossed the top of the fence and turned to look at Jim. "Listen," he said, "here's a job for you. You stay right there and watch for the pigs. Me and Darlene'll go in and get below them, and try to herd 'em up in this corner. As soon as you see any sign of them, you run get Mom, tell her what's going on. They'll be glad we rounded those pigs up. We won't press 'em hard, we'll just bring 'em up to this corner and hold 'em here, and Uncle Raymond can drop the gap and load them into his truck.

"Darlene, you come with me."

Billy worked his way down the far side of the fence, and I started up the near side. I couldn't tell whether what he said made sense or not, I was just responding to orders. My head felt funny and I had trouble climbing the fence, but finally I was over. Billy was waiting for me just inside the first row of corn.

"Okay," he said. "I'm going to go down the right side, and when I get to the bottom I'll start working across. You go out this way to the corner, and then go down about half way, and when you hear me whistle, start coming back in this direction. If you see any pigs, just go easy and keep 'em ahead of you." Billy grinned at me and whispered, "Let's hunt us a pig!" then turned and disappeared among the cornstalks.

I started to follow Billy, walked three or four rows deeper into the corn field, then stopped. I couldn't quite remember what Billy had said about going right, or going left. My eyes felt funny, and my tummy too, but at least it was cooler in here than back out there in the sunshine. I walked a little further into the corn, then looked around.

"Billy?" I whispered. "Billy?"

But the only sound was the soft snickering of the long leaves of corn. The hybrid field corn was tall; its tasseled tops waved far over my head. Here, deep among the plants, the air was dark and surprisingly cool. If I looked up, the gentle movement of the tassels seemed to snip the bright, distant sunlight into flickering bars and shafts that danced along the tops of the corn. I wandered farther among the rows of corn, occasionally lifting my gaze from the deep green of the stalks to the twinkling sunlight and brilliant blue sky among the tassels. The rows of corn were like an endless church congregation, all standing together as they sang hymn number... They were whispering, bending their yellow-gold heads to ask, which hymn? Which hymn? Was it the Doxology? Praise God from whom all blessing flow, they whispered. I started to sing too, Praise God from whom, then I remembered that I should be praying if I wanted to have a vision like Aunt Nellie, so I said, "Our Father Who art in Heaven."

Behind me someone said, "Umph."

It wasn't the dry, whispery voice of the corn, but a rough, gruff, old-man-clearing-his-throat sound.

"Hallowed by Thy Name," I said, and behind me someone said, "Umph, umph."

So I turned around slowly to see who was back there, and came chest-to-eye with one of Mr. Burcham's prize Hampshire hogs.

It was my chest and his eye, and he turned up his face for a more direct look. His eyes were little and dark, and his ears pointed forward, expressing an interested, curious attitude. The top of his head led directly into his great, rounded shoulders, which curved gracefully into his back and down into his haunches and ended in a tail that was longer than I thought pigs' tails were supposed to be and which he waved about like a friendly dog's. I could see the distinct, coarse hairs studding his great body, I could have reached out and touched them, and rubbed off some of the flaky dirt that coated his skin. He raised his nose to me, and the pink, flattened end of his snout tilted up and down, up and down. Then he gave a little toss of his head, just enough to flip the tips of his ears, and he said,

"Umph."

My reply was to lean forward and vomit all over his flat-ended snout and inquisitive ears.

The pig backed up a step and shook his head briskly.

I sank to my knees. All the rows of corn and the dancing sky and the golden tassels were shrinking and collapsing inward from all edges, until they were like a tiny round photograph, bright and clear, surrounded by total darkness. Just before the photograph winked out, its subject changed from a view of the corn field to a close-up of the face of a pig, and the pig face filled up my vision and spoke with a voice like muffled shotgun blasts. He said,

"R, I, P, Darlene."

That was the last I knew of this world or the next, until Mom was there, shaking me and wiping my face, and dimly I could hear Jimmy howling and Billy saying, over and over, "Is she dead, Mom? Is she dead? Mom, are you mad at me? It wasn't my fault."

"Sit up, Darlene," Mom said. "Billy, go get your brother and tell him to hush. Nobody's dead, Darlene just fainted."

Mom told me to just sit still for a minute, and she wiped the dirt and nastiness off my face and chest. I felt a lot better, and the corn didn't whisper like a congregation any more. I asked Mom what happened, and she said that I got too hot in the kitchen, and then drank too much green Kool Aid too fast. I'd be all right now, she said.

I sat and tried to remember what had happened. It all seemed so dreamy, I couldn't tell which parts were real. "Mom," I said, finally, "How did you know to come get me?"

"Billy found you here in the corn," she said. "He came and told me."

"Was there a pig with me when Billy found me?" I asked.

"He didn't say anything about a pig. Did you see one of Mr. Burcham's hogs in here?"

"I think so."

"Well, do you feel like walking to the house now? We'll tell Uncle Raymond about the pigs in his corn."

I felt a little wobbly and sort of light, like I weighed about half of what I normally did, but I made it to the house. Aunt Nellie made me lay down on the lounge chair on her back porch, and brought a big glass of water. She told me to drink it all, in sips, and she asked if I'd like a gingersnap. I told her no thanks, and she sat beside me while Mom went to gather up her things. It seemed like a good chance to find out some facts concerning visions.

"Aunt Nellie," I said, being careful to keep my voice a little weak, "do you believe children can be given a vision by God?"

"Of course," she answered.

"Are visions always writ large across the sky?" I don't know where I'd heard that phrase, but it had stuck in my head.

Aunt Nellie lowered her eyebrows and looked me right in the eye, but I gazed back with what I hoped was a pale, innocent air, and she answered, "Not necessarily."

I knew I was treading on thin ice, so I let the conversation go. On the way home I got to sit in the front seat, beside Mom, while the boys had to ride in the back and share the seat with a box of sixteen quarts of warm tomatoes. I scooted close to Mom and asked the one last thing I had to know.

"Mom," I said, "can a pig ever be trained to talk?"

"What?" Mom asked, surprised.

"You know, like a mynah bird. Could you ever train a pig to say people words?"

Mom laughed a little, softly, and the boys didn't hear. This was between just her and me. "No, Darlene, pigs can't talk."

"Not ever?" I whispered, "Not even if you trained them for a long time?"

"No, honey. It just can't happen. Their mouths and throats aren't made for it."

So there it was, plain as day. I knew I had heard a voice saying "R, I, P, Darlene," right when I was praying, and even if it had seemed to come out of a pig, a pig couldn't talk, so it must have been God. I'd been Touched by the Hand of God. I'd had a Vision.

It was too bad it happened in the middle of Uncle Raymond's corn field, with nobody there to witness it, and came by way of a big Hampshire hog upon which I had vomited green Kool Aid. And it was too bad that the message wasn't as interesting as Aunt Nellie's. But, all things considered, I felt pretty good about it. I was just a kid, and Aunt Nellie had been practicing for a long time. I figured that if I wanted to, I probably could work up to a real good vision by the time I was her age.

Getting Skeert

It was a cool day in early spring, and AJ and I were tearing old poplar siding off the interior walls of the run-down farmhouse we'd bought. I looked through the hole where the front door had hung and there was Coon Mabe standing on the front porch with his head stuck through the doorway. Coon gave me a scare. The house was nearly a mile off the gravel road, and people didn't just drop in unexpectedly. My hammer fell out of my hand like it had been pushed, and AJ turned to see what had happened.

"Hello!" he said to Coon, a tad too friendly. "What's happening?"

Coon stepped to the doorway and peered in, looking at AJ and at the mess. "That's what I come to ask. What is happening here? You a-tearing the place down?"

Coon looked like an old man, though he was only about fifty. He had on dirty bibbed overalls over a long-sleeved flannel shirt that was buttoned all the way up, and black Keds sneakers. He wore a feed store ball cap. It was what he wore every day, year 'round, except in winter he added a denim work jacket.

AJ walked to the doorway. I knew he was a little perturbed by this visitor. AJ thought we lived in splendid isolation, there on the farm. He thought because we didn't invite the neighbors in for dinner, nobody knew we were there.

"Well say, buddy, who are you?" AJ asked. He was smiling a big false smile, trying to cover up his worry, his little bit of fear. There were ten six-foot marijuana plants growing in a row behind the falling-down barn.

"I'm Coon Mabe. Who are you?" Coon looked AJ full in the face and waited.

"My name's AJ Gleason. This is my wife, Angela. We've bought this place."

"AJ. You've bought this place." Coon came in and started going from thing to thing in the deconstructed downstairs, keeping his hands clasped behind his back. He'd walk up to something laying in the floor, like a saw or a bag of nails, and he'd say "I know what that is," or "I don't know what that is," and move on to the next thing. Finally he got to Jolene, asleep in her basket, and he stopped, just stood there, looking. I moved to stand behind the basket and said, quietly so as not to wake her even though she'd learned to sleep through all but the worst of our remodeling racket, "That's Jolene. That's our baby."

He never looked up, but kept looking at the baby. After a few seconds, he said, "That's the baby," and he moved on to the next thing. A pile of lumber, trash swept into a pile, a crowbar. Those he knew. He didn't know what the stack of rolled fiberglass insulation was, or the red plastic cooler in which we'd stashed bottles of pop and beer and juice. But he didn't stop for explanations. It was like he was making a list.

AJ frowned at me behind Coon's back, casting significant glances from Coon to me and back. He wanted to know, did I know this person?

I finally said, "Coon's family has lived in Highlands County for about forever, haven't they, Coon? I believe their homeplace is up the creek from here, maybe a mile and a half. Does your brother still live with you, Coon?"

Everybody knew the Mabe family. Everybody knew about Coon.

"No, Brother moved away. Got married and moved away. Is

that baby dead?"

AJ frowned harder, exaggerating now, and I said, "No, that baby's just asleep. She'll wake up directly."

He didn't turn to look at me or AJ or the baby. He appeared to be examining the power saw near his feet. "I believe that must be some kind of a saw," he said softly, and nodded his head. "It's got a blade. Be careful with blades."

"Hey, Coon," AJ said, talking loudly, genially, "How did you get here? Did you walk? I didn't hear a truck drive up."

Coon didn't look at AJ, but in a few seconds he said, "I walked. I heerd your racket."

AJ started to catch on. He started to not worry about the pot, began to smile and feel in charge again. He winked at me. "How about a drink, Coon? We've got some juice in the cooler, there."

Coon looked up immediately, and spoke in a louder tone. "I love pop. Do you have pop? Pepsi's my fav'rite."

"Well, I think we just might have a Pepsi in here. Let's see. Here you go. Grab this can, my man, and let's go sit on the porch and take a little break. You've walked a long way, and I've been work-ing hard, and hard-working men like us deserve a break now and then, don't we?"

Coon smiled at AJ. "Yes sir! You and me's hard workers!" He grabbed the can of Pepsi and tugged at the pull ring, and only spilled a little when it came open. AJ grinned at me again and pat-ted Coon on the back, and they went out to sit on the porch. I got a can of juice from the cooler and picked up Jolene's basket and went out the back door with it balanced on my hip. I couldn't put my finger on why, but I didn't like watching AJ talking to Coon. I went out and pulled weeds out of our garden, and when I heard old nails being pulled from dry wood, I knew Coon was gone and AJ was back at work. I went in to help.

We spent that spring and summer scraping by, living off what AJ made as a rough carpenter and what I generated selling the wooden shingles off the barn. I painted pictures of log cabins or mountains or chickadees or cardinals on the shingles, and they sold steadily at $5 to $6. We made friends with people in the health food co-op, and with some of the people AJ worked with and even with one or two he worked for.

AJ really got into being the great mountaineer. He dug a pond in the back yard, but it never would hold water. The most it did was provide muddy bathing for the ducks and geese he brought home. He bought six goats to eat down the brush he didn't have time to cut, but the goats decided they'd rather live on our front porch than out in the wilderness, and since there were no fences on earth that could hold them, they had the run of the place, including the porch swing and rocking chair and my herb garden and flower beds, until AJ traded them for a cow.

The cow died three weeks later, after the vet paid a $125 visit to tell us she was going to. We ordered day-old chicks from a hatchery in Indiana, and when they turned out to be 98% roosters, AJ decided we'd butcher them and "put them up," the way old-timers did. So I canned forty-two quarts of chicken, not one bite of which I could eat. The smell turned my stomach.

All through those days, Coon Mabe hovered around the edges of our lives. He liked to show up at the front door early in the morning, just after dawn. He'd yell and wake us up, and expect us to open the door and let him in. Finally AJ told him the children liked to sleep late, and Coon's yelling woke them - though it wasn't really the kids who wanted to sleep in. After that, Coon would just sit on the porch and wait. He wouldn't even rock in the rocking chair, for fear the creaking would disturb "the babies."

Coon loved to go in the truck with AJ. Sometimes he would think up reasons why he needed to go to the store, and he'd ask AJ to take him, and sometimes he'd just ask, in a man-to-man tone, if AJ was going to the store that day because if he was, he believed he'd ride along with him. If Coon had any money left from his Social Security check, he'd offer to buy gas for the truck, and AJ always took it, which drove me nuts.

"Why are you taking money from that poor old man?" I asked.

"Why not? He'd just spend it on something else, and I take him to the store, don't I?"

"Yeah, when you're going anyway."

"So? Look, he doesn't even remember where his money goes. Why not let a little of it run through my truck? He loves that truck.

Him and Brenda, I don't know which of them loves to go riding in the truck the most. All I have to do is open the door, both of them are in there like scrap iron on a magnet."

Brenda was AJ's dog.

I invited Coon to eat with us. One day he showed me a cut he'd gotten on his shin and I was startled not by the scrape but by the thinness of his leg. His overalls and long-sleeved shirts covered most of him up, but underneath them, he was skin and bones.

"Why, Coon," I said without thinking, "you're so thin! No wonder you got a scrape when you fell, there's no padding on that leg."

"It hurt, but I believe I'll be all right," he said, dropping his pants leg.

"Yes, I think your cut will be fine. But you need to gain a little weight, Coon. What do you like to eat?"

"Moon Pies. I like them Moon Pies."

That's what Coon bought when AJ took him to the store. "Yes, I know you like Moon Pies, but what do you like to eat for lunch, Coon?" I thought I'd fix something he liked and feed it to him, right then and there.

Coon looked away and didn't answer.

"Coon?" I prodded. Then I thought, maybe he doesn't use the word "lunch." "What do you like to eat for supper?"

"For supper I eat Spam. Spam's for supper."

"Do you eat Spam for supper every night, Coon?"

"Spam's for supper."

I hung my head for a minute. Then I asked, "Do you like chicken, Coon? I've got some nice leftover chicken. I could make dumplings, do you like chicken and dumplings?"

"Chicken makes my belly hurt."

"Would you like a hamburger, Coon? I could fry you a hamburger."

"Hamburger makes my belly hurt."

"Coon, what do you like to eat? I'll fix something you like, and you can have supper with us, okay?"

"Reckon I'll get on home. Gotta get going."

Later I talked to AJ about it, but AJ just laughed. "That old man will outlive you and me both, Ang. He's slim and trim, and he walks everywhere. We'll die with clogged arteries when we're fifty, and Coon Mabe will walk to our funerals. If he can't bum a ride in somebody's pickup."

"But I don't believe he's eating right. Have you ever seen him eat anything but Moon Pies, or drink anything but Pepsi?"

"Quit worrying, Angela. Coon has the world by the tail. He doesn't worry about paying bills or keeping up with the Joneses. Hell, Coon Mabe is the epitome of that to which we should all aspire. He lives life in the moment, like Buddha says. Coon Mabe, an enlightened man!"

AJ laughed, and later I heard him repeat this to his friends. I even heard him say it in front of Coon, with his arm thrown around Coon's skinny shoulders. Everybody laughed.

No matter how often I asked him, or what I offered, Coon wouldn't eat with us. I finally quit asking.

One October day I woke up and realized that we had been on the farm for seven months. Crystal had started kindergarten a few weeks earlier. My mother had taken the baby for a couple of days, and I had finally caught up on the gardening. AJ and two of his cronies were working on the barn, turning it into a woodworking shop. They had a six-pack of beer apiece, so I knew they wouldn't miss me. I had a sudden urge to get to a high place, to take a look around and see what the world looked like. I had been on that farm with my head bent, digging as hard as I could just to keep from getting covered up, for a long time. I had a sudden feeling like I was rising up out of deep water, and I wanted to get higher.

I walked to the barn. "AJ," I said, "I'm going to drive up on the ridge for a while. I'll be back before Crystal gets home from school."

He was hammering a big nail through a two-by-four, attaching it to a sill he'd laid on top of the old pine flooring. "Where are you going?" he asked, still whacking with the hammer.

"Razor Ridge, I guess." I raised my voice, to get it over the noise. "I think I'll take my watercolor stuff, see if I still know how to make a picture."

"I didn't know you were an artist, Angela," Bobby said. He'd been working on the crew with AJ for a couple of months.

"I used to be, about a lifetime ago," I muttered, but then I added, louder, "There's plenty of sandwich stuff, ya'll help yourselves to lunch."

AJ stopped hammering and looked at me. He smiled, but I could tell he was not thrilled with me taking off like this. "Just because the kids are not here, doesn't mean you're not needed," he said.

"Tell you what," Dick added. Dick was a friend of AJ's, a Vietnam vet whose live-in told me he still slept with a big knife under his pillow. He didn't talk a lot, and when he did I was never sure if he was serious or pulling somebody's leg. "You'd better not wander far from your car, up on Razor. I was down at the store yesterday, and all the old geezers were talking about the bear they've been seeing up there."

I raised my eyebrows, but Dick just smiled and turned back to work.

But Bobby chimed in. "Oh hell yeah, Carl Young said he'd seen it three or four times. He claims it's an old she-bear, raised cubs up around the High Tree Rock this summer."

I looked at AJ, but all he did was look back and grin.

"Well," I smiled at all of them together. "I'll keep a sharp eye out. I'd enjoy seeing a bear. There hasn't been a reliable sighting in Highlands County in fifty years." I waved and left.

I loaded a big tablet of paper, a handful of cheap brushes squeezed together in a rubber band, and a quart jar of water into a box with my old tubes of watercolors. Probably half of them would be dried out, but I wasn't nearly as interested in painting as I was in getting out, and up. By then I was craving it like a field hand craves dinner. It almost bent me over, I wanted it so bad.

The way up Razor Ridge is a narrow gravel road with a lot of steep grade and several switchbacks, and I kept shooting glances into the brush on either side, checking bear-shaped shadows, but when I got to the top I had no doubts about whether I should have come. There is a place up there where the ridges fall away from the road to the southeast, and they go on and on. They were in their fall colors, the deep dusty red of oaks and the bright yellows of poplars. Mason's Ridge stood out with its dark stand of hemlock, and far off, at some place way down in North Carolina, the hills turned to smoky blue, like the bloom on a damson, and then faded and faded until at last the sky folded down around them.

I stood there looking at the hills, and I began to take deep, deep breaths, and blow them out slowly. I closed my eyes and tilted my face, so the sun shined right down on it. Every time I'd breathe in, I could smell the dust of the road and the different dust of the pasture field and underneath that the spicy smell of dry leaves and even, way down, a cool hint of Charlie's Creek, rolling down the holler nearly a quarter-mile below. After many deep breaths I got my painting stuff out of the car and crawled under the fence into the field. I sat down and started playing with the colors, washing browns and reds together up to a dry edge, then adding a swipe of dark opaque green at the top.

Behind me, something snorted.

My hand jerked and shot the tablet out of my lap. The quart of water turned on its side and started a long roll to the bottom of Razor Ridge. Wrinkled tubes of watercolor paint scattered in a fan around my feet as I whirled to see what was back there.

"Coon Mabe!" Coon grinned, but my heart was beating on my ribs like a sledge hammer on a wedge, and anger flew up in a storm. "Shit! What do you think you're doing?"

"Was ye skeert?"

"Was I skeert? Was I skeert ? Why, you fool, of course I was scared! I could've had a heart attack. Jesus Christ, Coon, what ever made you do that? How'd you get up here, anyway?" I was mad, but I was starting to get my breath back, too, and already I was ashamed of yelling at him. I bent over and gathered up the tubes of paint. I had to go down three or four steps to retrieve the paper, and I stood there with my hand shading my eyes, looking for the jar.

I decided it was long gone, and turned to start up the hill to the car. I took a step or two, then glanced at Coon's face. He was sitting on the grass on the road side of the barbed wire fence, looking my way, and he looked bad.

"Oh Coon, don't worry about it. I'm sorry I yelled at you."

"AJ said it would be funny."

"AJ said, huh?" That was typical. But Coon looked really sad, so I added, "It was kinda funny, wasn't it? Did you see me jump?"

Coon smiled, a little. I climbed to the fence and crawled under. I went to the opposite side of the car to load the art supplies, then stood for a minute with my hand on the front door handle. I was ready to go, but it would be rude to drive off and leave Coon sitting on the side of Razor Ridge. At the very least, I ought to offer him a ride back to the house. I stood in the sun and waited for my mouth to say the words, but nothing came out.

The truth of the matter was, I had never been alone with Coon Mabe before, and I was uneasy. During my childhood my only contact with him had been to watch him walking along the county roads. Since we'd moved to the farm and he'd become a frequent visitor to our house, I'd kept a little distance between me and Coon. I'd always been polite, but I'd never really wanted him to get too comfortable in our house.

Just like I didn't really want him to sit in my car with me.

It hurt me, to let these feelings come to the light. I tried to keep them packed back in the dark corners of my mind, but the light on the Ridge was too clear, too bright. It shined down on the superiority I'd secretly felt towards AJ, who treated Coon the same way he treated the dog, and lit up the little nugget of disgust I'd kept back there for Coon.

I didn't want to know this. I wanted to be the good guy, especially when it came to this poor old man. Admitting those feelings was like rubbing something nasty into the golden glow I'd gotten, up there on the Ridge. But once I'd seen the truth, I couldn't unknow it. In my head, the fall sunshine focused like the beam of a movie camera, and projected a series of little vignettes: me standing between Coon and the baby; me standing behind the hooked screen door, telling Coon that AJ was not there; me warning the children not to get too close to Coon; me offering Coon food, but not persuading him to eat. Over and over, dozens of variations on the theme of be nice, but don't be close.

From where I was standing I could see the corner of Coon's shoulder, behind the rear fender of the car. He hadn't moved. I stood with my eyes closed for a minute, cursing silently. I called up every dirty word I knew, every one I'd ever heard, and with every one of them I begged, don't make me do this. But no great celestial voice boomed out, Okay, forget it. So I walked around the front of the car, back to where he was. I sat down near him.

He was looking out at the hills, just as I'd done that morning.

"Coon," I said, "I'm not mad. You scared me good, that's all."

He smiled at me and said, "Well," then turned back to the hills.

"I'm sorry I yelled at you."

"That's all right."

He was quiet for such a long time, I finally asked, "Coon, are you feeling okay?"

"I'm a little tired," he said, and I looked carefully at his face because I'd never heard him make any kind of complaint, before. Of course, I'd never asked, before. Under the stubble of individual, whitish whisker stubs, Coon's cheeks were dipped and eroded with deep wrinkles that ran from cheekbones to jaw. His skin was a gray color that, if I'd seen it on the face of one of my children, would mean I'd shortly be cleaning up a mess.

"Are you going to vomit?" I hurriedly asked.

"No." He spoke quietly, still gazing at the hills.

I checked again, and saw that his hands were pale, too, and a little shaky even as they lay on his knees. But there was no sheen of perspiration on his lip or forehead. In fact, his skin seem un-naturally dry. I looked at him and thought for a few seconds, then asked, "Did you walk all the way up here?"

"AJ brought me to the foot of the Ridge." From the foot of the Ridge to where we sat was two miles of the steepest road in Highlands County. Bless AJ's heart. But now I really had no choice.

"Come on, Coon, let's get in my car and we'll go back to the house."

It took Coon a few seconds to muster up the strength to say, "I believe I'll just stay."

I'd never been able to bring myself to invite Coon Mabe to sit in my car before, and now here he was, turning me down. I stood up. "Come on, Coon, you can tell AJ I'm a better driver than he is."

Instead of answering, Coon slowly leaned forward until his

forehead rested against the fencepost near his knee.

"Coon! Come on, man. We've got to get you down from here."

Very softly he said, "Believe I'll just stay."

Now I was scared. I squatted beside him, and saw that his eyes were closed, but he was breathing. I reached out and put my hand on his elbow, and shook it a little, and spoke like I would have to Crystal, to get her out of bed in time to catch the bus. I told him to come on, I promised him ice cream, I told him that he and AJ would have a good time laughing about how he'd scared me. I said that I had been sure I was about to be eaten by a bear, right there on Razor Ridge. I said everything I could think of, and finally lifted him by putting my hands under his arms and pulling up, and laid him up against me and mostly carried and a little bit helped him walk around my car. I loaded him into the back and then I drove off Razor Ridge in half the time it normally took, clawing around curves on the wrong side and scattering gravel. I went straight to the clinic in Hillton, and the whole way I talked and talked to him, and he didn't answer.

When we got there I took a quick look at Coon, but I wasn't sure he was still alive. I ran into the building and told the nurse to hurry. She got a doctor and they went to the car and checked Coon and even though they didn't say so, I knew he was not dead, because they worked on him a little, and asked me some questions about him that I didn't have answers for. Finally the nurse went back in and in a few minutes an ambulance pulled up. The attendants loaded Coon into it and then swept out to the main road and that was it. I had given the doctor the name of Coon's brother, and that was all I could do, they said. I should go home.

So I went home, and told AJ and Bobby and Dick what had happened, and asked why they'd sent Coon all that way. It was just a joke, they said, you know Coon, always glad to be in on a joke. Or the butt of one, I thought, but couldn't say. Yesterday I could have. Back then, I'd been the good guy.

We heard they put Coon, whose real name turned out to be John Delano Mabe, into a nursing home. He was suffering from malnutrition and dehydration. Turns out, all he ever ate was Moon Pies and Spam and crackers. He drank Pepsis. He lived for a couple of months there, and then passed away in his sleep.

The kids remember Coon, and talk about him, sometimes. I always tell them he was a man who never asked a lot for himself, and remind them that his real name was John, which, according to the Scriptural Directory in the back of AJ's family Bible, means gift of God.

Tomato Jam

The phone rings, and I sigh but answer it anyway. I know who it is and I know how long she'll talk and I just about know what she's going to say. She calls two or three times a week, always pretty much the same thing. I need to get some work done this morning, I've got to go by school and pick up Randy and get him into town before the library closes this afternoon, and there's the last of the tomatoes needing to be dealt with, but I go ahead and answer it. I can peel tomatoes and talk at the same time.

"Hello," I say.

"Good morning, Mary, what are you into today?"

"Hey Dariene. I'm working up some tomatoes, here."

"Do you still have tomatoes? The last of mine dried up two weeks ago."

"I've got a few. I thought I'd turn them into tomato jam, Jack likes it so."

"Tomato jam? I never heard of tomato jam. How do you make it?"

And off we go. Darlene and I have been friends for years, ever since I sat in front of her in high school English class and let her copy off my papers. Then we had biology together and I couldn't understand diddly about it, and she helped me along although I never did exactly copy her work. She just talked me through the experiments, sort of. And then I talked her through when she ran off and married David, and when the glamour wore off my marriage to Jack, she talked me through it and helped me fall in love with him all over again. We've talked each other through being pregnant, two times each, and through ear infections and broken collarbones and underachieving and hormone-y teenagers.

We don't get to see each other in person as much as we used to, which is kind of funny, considering we just live about three miles apart. And when we do visit in person, it's usually not as good, not as comfortable and easy, as talking over the phone. We have a real telephone relationship, I tell people. I can bare my heart to Darlene-the-voice even better than to Darlene-the-real-person. And I can get some work done at the same time.

After all these years of calling each other back and forth, she knows everything there is to know about me. She knows about the only man other than Jack I ever slept with, and nobody and I mean NOBODY else knows that, because the guy died years ago, and it was only him and me in on that secret, that's a fact. She knows the exact ways my mother can drive me crazy, and she knows when I start my periods. She knows when Jack and I get in an argument, and she knows what to say to make me feel better. She knows it all.

And I know all about her, too. About her kids and her mother and about her daddy getting killed in the war before she was even born, and being brought up by aunts and cousins. I know about her husband, David, how she nearly left him once, years ago, and then decided she couldn't because she didn't have enough money and she didn't want to have to go to work and put the baby in day-care. So she stuck it out and they got all right again, and are like a foot in an old shoe, now, comfortable and fitted to each other.

I know her family history for at least two generations, because Darlene is a big talker, and doesn't mind airing the family laundry.

I love her dearly, and if something significant is going on in either of our lives, I pay attention like interest to a bank, but when things are dull she can use up a lot of my time just talking about nothing. So I've developed a whole list of work I can get done while Darlene's talking to me.

I prop the receiver between my ear and shoulder, and get out a saucepan to heat water. I set it on the stove, turn the knob to "high," get another pan for ice water. Darlene is saying,

"...this was my Aunt Alta's second son, the only one in that whole bunch who never amounted to much. I mean, you remember my Aunt Alta, she's the one who had nine kids before her husband died, and she raised them all by being a home health nurse? She raised those kids up by the nape of the neck, you know, just any way she could, I mean here she was, a woman on her own back in the forties, I guess she did well to keep them fed and in shoes, but it was pretty rough for those kids, I remember that. And Aunt Alta is so flighty. You wouldn't think a woman who was a nurse and looked after sick people could be so light in her loafers, but I swear, Aunt Alta takes the cake. She's the one who told David that if he ever was in a accident and got an arm or a leg cut off, to make sure they buried it before the sun went down, or it would hurt him for the rest of his life. Can you believe that?"

I laugh as I put the first five tomatoes in the hot water, then pull out the drawer to find the big slotted spoon. You shouldn't leave tomatoes in the hot water for more than just a second, or they'll start cooking. Before you know it, you'll have mush.

"But you know, the strange thing is, every one of those kids except Albert did real well. Every one of the nine went to college, they could get financial assistance because Uncle Ross was killed in war time, and every one of them went and really made something of themselves. But Albert was the one that all the relatives would say, 'That Albert, he's as smart as he can be, but he just don't have any sense.' I mean, in a way, it wasn't all that big a surprise when he fell off that dam and got killed."

That's the thing about Darlene. If nothing worth talking about is going on in her life at the moment, lots of stuff has happened in the past, and she isn't adverse to bringing it up again. I start peeling the first tomatoes. It is a pleasure to skin ripe tomatoes. After you dip them in hot water and then in ice water, the skins split and just seem to want to come off. Lots of times you can slip them off with just your fingers. Other times, you have to catch the start of them between your thumb and the blade of your paring knife, but it is almost a thrill, the way it pulls off so easy and yet so firm, with a soft, whispery separating sound.

"Yeah, I remember you telling me about him getting killed," I say, and listen to the skin pulling away from the flesh of the tomato. It gives me a feeling up my spine, like somebody peeling off a big piece of sunburned skin from my back.

"Well, that was years ago, he died back when my kids were small, but anyway, Momma called this morning and while we were talking, she remembered the time when Albert got a good one on his mother-in-law."

This sounds like it will take a while. Darlene's family has as many connections and stories as a hound has fleas. But I've got plenty of tomatoes.

"She was living with them, and Albert never did like her. She was bossy, and was always getting on to Albert about stuff, and you know how it is when relatives move in.

"And the worst thing was, the only place they could fix up for her room was the room that used to be the den. And the only way to get to the bathroom was through the den. So any time Albert had to go to the bathroom he had to walk right through old Mrs. Cooper's bedroom, and since Albert slept in the nude - I'm sure every one of Aunt Alta's children sleeps naked right to this day, Momma says they didn't have enough flour sacks to make nightgowns when they were growing up so they all developed the habit of sleeping bare - it was a big torment to him to get up in the middle of the night to pee, because he'd have to get dressed and walk through the old lady's room, with her asleep right there. The commode was right on the other side of the wall where she had the head of her bed, and he just knew she could hear him peeing and he felt like he shouldn't fart or anything. It annoyed him no end."

I measure out peeled, chopped tomatoes into my big kettle, then measure sugar into a bowl and set it by. It takes four and a half cups of sugar for every three cups of tomatoes. That sounds like a lot of sugar, but you add a fourth-cup of lemon juice and two teaspoons of grated lemon peel to the tomatoes, and it takes a lot of sweetening to overcome that much sour.

"Well, I can understand why," I say, mostly just to show I'm listening. "I'd hate to have to go through somebody else's bedroom to get to the bathroom, too."

"Oh, I know it. But then Albert figured out that Mrs. Cooper was deaf as a post, and slept like a log, to boot. Plus, she had a pair of those glasses like people used to have to wear after they'd had cataract surgery, which she'd had, and you know, without those glasses they couldn't see much of nothing. And she had the habit of taking off her glasses and her false teeth and setting them both, side by side, on top of the dresser, which was on the other side of the room, before she got into bed. So Albert realized she probably wouldn't wake up if he went through there at night, and if she did wake up she couldn't hear him or see well enough to know if he was naked or not, and so he went back to just strolling through in the natural, and letting loose with whatever in the bathroom. You know, it probably gave him a little satisfaction, to think he was mooning the old lady and she didn't even know it."

I laugh again. God knows, such small pleasures as mooning your mother-in-law are what makes it all worthwhile. I add seasonings to the tomatoes and lemon: 1/2 teaspoon allspice, 1/2 teaspoon cinnamon, 1/4 teaspoon cloves. I stir in a box of SureJell, and set it on the stove to bring to a boil. As it warms up I smell the combination of tomatoes and spices and lemon, and my tongue curls up along its edges. Not many people like tomato jam the way Jack does. It's a strange combination of flavors, sort of on the order of ketchup, but not so smooth. Jack says it's his favorite thing on a hot buttered biscuit.

"So Momma said, one night Albert was on his way to the bathroom, naked as a jaybird, and when he was going past that chest of drawers, he happened to look over and see her false teeth setting there. And he had this idea. He stopped walking, reached out and picked up those teeth, and used them to scratch his butt. Just scratched it big time, all around and right down next to the crack and everything. Then he laid those teeth back on the bureau, and he went on to the bathroom and then went back to bed. And I reckon the whole thing would never have been found out, but he was so tickled by it that when he got back in bed, he kept laughing."

By now I am laughing too. Finally I catch my breath, sniff, and say, "So what happened?"

"Well, Momma said that Aunt Doris asked him what he was laughing about, but he wouldn't tell. And finally Aunt Doris got mad and got up out of bed and slept the rest of the night on the couch. When Albert got up the next morning, Doris and her mother were already up and dressed, with their coats and hats on and a bag by Mrs. Cooper's feet.

"And Aunt Doris said, 'Albert, I've had about all of your childish behavior I'm going to take. First you grumble and sulk like a spoiled child because Mother comes to stay with us for a little while, and then you keep me up all hours of the night, giggling, and won't even tell me why.'

'Why, Doris, what do you mean, a little while? She's been here for eight months already, and she's not showing any signs of leaving.'

"Well, that made Aunt Doris even madder, and she huffed up and said that if Albert didn't explain, she'd go on back home with Mother. And the whole time Doris and Albert were talking, Mrs. Cooper was sitting right there beside Doris, smiling with those false teeth in her mouth, and every time Uncle Albert glanced at her he'd want to laugh so bad he couldn't hardly stand it, until finally he broke down. Once he started he couldn't stop, and Doris and her mother went out the door while Uncle Albert was down on all fours, laughing."

By now I have added the sugar to the tomato mixture, brought it to a full rolling boil, and counted down the minute it needed to cook. The jam needs to be poured into jars, but this is too tricky to do while keeping the telephone receiver in position and keeping up with Darlene's voice. So I say, "Darlene, can you hold on for just a minute?"

"Sure," she says. I lay the phone down and pour up the jam. Six little jars, it only takes a few seconds. I slap on the lids, tighten the bands, turn them all upside down.

"Okay," I say, "I'm back. So what happened to Uncle Albert

and Aunt Doris?"

"Well, they eventually got back together. They had four kids after that, and were taking them on a big vacation out west, when Albert fell off the Hoover Dam. Momma said everybody just knew Doris would have to farm those kids out among the relatives, because she hadn't ever worked and didn't know how to do a thing in this world but make coconut cakes and serve on church committees, but come to find out, Albert had a great big life insurance policy, plus her mother died not two months after Albert fell, and left everything she had to Doris and the kids, so they were in pretty good shape, for long enough for Doris to take the nurses' training course, anyway."

"No kidding!" I say. "So Albert did pretty well after all. But how did your Momma ever learn about the false teeth?"

"That's the funniest thing of all," Darlene says. "Aunt Doris knew about them all along. She told Momma about it years later, long after Uncle Albert and Mrs. Cooper were dead and gone. She said she'd gotten up to go to the bathroom, too, and was waiting at the door to the den when Albert stopped and scratched his butt with those dentures. She said she couldn't believe he'd do that, and then she thought about it and had to admit it was pretty funny. But she was afraid that if he ever told anybody about it, she'd never be able to show her face again, so she created that whole scene just to see how far she had to push him before he'd admit it."

"And how far did she push?"

"Well, she took her mother home and stayed with her for three days, and Albert called and asked her to come back, but absolutely refused to tell her what had happened that night. So Doris figured he'd never tell anybody, and she went back to Albert and left her mother to take care of herself. And they must have gotten along pretty well, because they had those four kids in the next six years, and then he died two years later and Doris never remarried or went back to stay with her mother, even when her mother had to be put in a nursing home."

"Well," I say, "I guess I'd better clean up my mess here in the kitchen."

"You know," Darlene says, " they put Mrs. Cooper in the same nursing home that we had to put David's mother in."

"You had to put David's mother in a nursing home?" I ask, even though I don't want to start another story, even though I have not heard this one before.

"Oh yes. She was so old, you know. And the funny thing was -"

"Darlene," I interrupt, "I've got to go, I hear Jack's car in the driveway, and I need to get this jam off the counter." So we hang up, and Jack comes in for lunch, and later I put the jars of tomato jam on the shelves in the laundry room. And when I have them all arranged, in neat, shining rows between the grape jelly and the apple pie filling, I get the telephone and push the automatic dial button for Darlene's number. Because Darlene and I talk each other through almost everything, dead uncles or jars of jam or whatever.

Chimera

I can picture us as we were then, little more than a year ago. It does seem longer, but that's because life in this back-of-nowhere place usually slips along easily, one week much like the week before, the ones and couples of us in our routines of meetings and trips to town, hobbies, volunteer hours for our various good works. It's as if we are all winding down our lives, easing into old age, accepting dullness along with security, and with that acceptance and sameness comes a lack of ways to mark off time. Without interesting events and activities and people to make a time or place significant, the days and weeks melt into one another. Time drags and stretches: a day seems long; a week, endless; a year can seem almost like a lifetime.

But once, before this past year of emptiness, our lives were marked by an event that made us all feel fully aware, that made us look hard at who we were and who we thought we were. That event made us realize that sometimes things are not really what they seem to be; not only what they seem to be.

We used to get together regularly to do hand work and talk. Linda and Elaine came mostly for the talk; Pam always had her knitting, and I had whatever quilting project was current. I like quilting; I am not one of the new generation of art quilters, and I am not an old-fashioned, make-it-practical, tack it and use it, quilter. Somewhere in between, I quilt as much for the therapy of the work as for the pleasure of the product. I find it soothing to organize and plan, stitch and join.

I finished more projects in those days. It helped to have the meetings to plan for, to encourage me to get things done and ready for when the others came over. I always needed to have a project at a point where Linda and Pam could work on it: something in the frames or pieces to cut.

Pam is first to arrive, as usual. Between her need to get her car as close to the house as possible and her desire to be able to leave whenever she wants without making somebody move a car or two, parking closest to the house always wins. I hear a vehicle pull up the driveway, glance through the curtains to affirm that it is, indeed, Pam, and continue to slide the dustmop under the couch. I'll have a few minutes between Pam's arrival and her call at the back door.

I push the dust mop (loaded with hairy dust rolls) into the laundry room, put a kettle of water on the stove and turn on the heat under it, then go to the back door and look out. Pam is working her way up the three steps.

I ask, "Can I help?" Pam was diagnosed with MS ten years ago. She's "done well," as the doctors tell her at every visit. It makes me mad at the entire medical establishment, to know what they consider "well."

"No," Pam drawls. "Just give me a few minutes to rest along the way." She moves her hands up the handrail, grasps it tightly, and pulls her right leg up to the next step.

"Here. Let me take your bag." I hold her cane until the bag is out of the way, then return it to Pam's left hand. "Nice stick."

"Yeah, Fred got me a new one. He said it would match the Clementines' new outfits."

"So Fred is being the dutiful son this week?"

"F-t-t-t-t-t. He probably charged the cane on my credit card."

"Ha." I am careful to keep my voice lightly sarcastic. Fred

might be a bum, but he is Pam's only son, and I know better than to be too critical.

Pam pauses to catch her breath on the second step. "So, is everybody else coming?"

"As far as I know."

When Pam is in the house and settled on the couch, I finish setting out the extra quilting tools they'll need: more scissors, another spool of thread, a couple of rulers and marking pencils. As I am positioning two more chairs around the quilting frame, we hear more cars crunching gravel in the driveway. I don't expect my friends to wait to be let in, and soon the voices of two more women float through to us.

"Helloooooooooo! It's us."

"Come on in, Us," I answer. I can hear Linda's rich, Yankee-flavored voice murmuring, followed by Elaine's higher-pitched, cheery voice answering, "Well, I'm not sure. You know I'd love to concentrate on my windows? But we need the income?"

It is Elaine's habit to end almost every sentence tentatively, with at least an implied question mark. Her friends accuse her of letting her childhood in the Deep South corrupt her in several ways, the most obvious being her speaking style.

Elaine and Linda deposit hugs and sweaters around the room, set down their bags, smooth their hands over the surface of the pieced quilt stretched in the frame, and comment on how much I've gotten done since the last time we worked together. They continue to talk, sharing information about families and the community, while I fill an insulated carafe with boiling water, set the carafe on an already prepared tray, and return with it to the sewing room.

"Okay, tea and zucchini bread are here. Help yourselves, and remember that any stains on the quilt mean you owe me endless hours of cheerful, un-begrudged labor on whatever project I choose."

"Good lord, with a deal like that, you must be dying for someone to have a little accident," Pam muttered.

"You bet." I get my mug of Earl Grey and settle in my usual place at the bottom of the quilt. I sip, set the mug on the floor near my foot, and slip a thimble onto the middle finger of my right hand. A threaded needle is waiting in front of me. I like to end a quilting session by threading a needle, setting it into position, pulling the knot through the top layer of the quilt, and taking just one needle's-length of stitches. This means the next session can begin with simply picking up the needle and starting to sew, without threading, positioning, or other delays. It gets a session off to a good start, and allows me to make "sessions" out of any stolen blocks of time, no matter how brief.

"I swear, this is a beautiful quilt," Linda says, leaning back and looking at the quilt through half-opened eyes. "Are you sure you want my ugly stitches on it?"

"Get to work," I order.

"She won't let you get out of it as easily as that," Pam says from her place on the couch. Pam isn't a quilter. She introduces herself to newcomers as "a singer, a homemaker, and a talker, in that order." She always brings a knitting project to our get-togethers.

Without responding to the entirely rhetorical exchange, Linda selects one of the already-threaded needles stuck into the pincushion near her, and takes her first stab in the fabric in front of her.

At the side of the quilt opposite to Pam, Elaine holds a needle in her fingers and looks at the quilt top. "Now, how did you want this design to go? On the side here, do you want the scallops pointing up?"

"Yeah, like you'd do a decoration on a hem." I slide a paper template and a chalk pencil across to Elaine. Then, when Elaine hesitates, I move to her side of the quilt, position the paper slightly above the edge of the quilt, and quickly chalk along the pattern's edge. "Like that. And you know how I am. You don't have to be exact," I add. Elaine sometimes obsesses over details to the point of getting absolutely nothing done, so it is best to get her started.

The women settle into work, each finding a rhythm that soothes and satisfies her. We have realized, over our years of working together, that a few minutes' silence at the beginning of our "meetings" means our time together is more productive and more harmonious. In other settings, we can out-talk the best socialites; in the company of our husbands, we seldom let a moment's silence fall. But these twice-a-month working visits are different. They are at once more casual and intimate, and more formalized than any other of our times together. Without anyone consciously organizing them, our work sessions have settled into a format.

We usually met at my house, which is more or less centrally located and has good parking. Also, I am the most serious about my work, and I have large, old-fashioned quilting frames and room in which to set them up and leave them for weeks at a stretch. By then we almost never met at Pam's house; no one ever said it out loud, but we all knew that her claim to be a painstaking homemaker, although well-founded for the first 25 years of her marriage, was not true since the MS had taken its toll on her body – and since death had taken her husband. She'd have been embarrassed to have us see it. Elaine's house was too small. Occasionally we gathered at Linda's house. We all enjoyed sitting in her pretty, sweetly decorated living room, but there each woman had to work on her own, individual project, since there wasn't enough room to set up a group project. There's something about working together (not just in the same room) that conduces the bond of friendship, so most of our work sessions took place here. I liked it that way.

And, after settling in, the meetings begin in silence. Once the atmosphere is established and the work well underway, we'll talk about whatever anyone wants. Luckily, we are generally alike in politics, so that subject is often explored. And religion is something we've discussed in detail, although our preferences on that subject range from the conservative and formalized to the vaguest New Age "airy-fairy crap" imaginable. Still, we've agreed and disagreed and managed to support each other's beliefs through marriages (even seconds and a third), divorces, unruly toddlers and irrational teenagers, births and deaths and failing parents, financial successes and failures, and our own and our husbands' midlife crises.

I cherish these times together, and assume the others feel the same. That's assumed rather than discussed because I have – I admit it, after a teenaged life filled with Tolkien's hobbits and wizards – a touch of superstition in me. I've never broached the topic because I have a feeling that to talk about it would be setting it up to be changed. Bringing it out into the open would have jinxed it.

Maybe.

Thinking about that, I sneak looks at the friends who are seated around the quilt spread in the frames. What binds us together? I wonder. Who'd pick us out of a lineup, to be such long-time friends? There's twenty years' differences in our ages, a quarter of a continent's distance between our childhood homes, thousands of dollars' gaps in our incomes, and yet here we are. Singer, teacher, secretary, and I don't know how you'd really classify Linda. Piano teacher? Perpetual newlywed? I feel myself smiling as I weave my needle through the layers of backing, batting and pieced top of the quilt. There is a soft "pop" as the end of the needle pulls out of the cloth, then a quiet "zzzzzzip" as I pull the thread through, leaving behind six tiny, new stitches. I position the point of the needle in front of the last stitch and start the process again. Weave, pop, pull, sigh.

Ten or fifteen minutes pass before anyone speaks. Finally, without lifting my head from its tilt over the quilt, I ask, "What are the Clementines going to wear for their gig Saturday night?"

The Clementines is Pam's "almost-a cappella" singing group. As her multiple sclerosis has progressed, the group has curtailed its public appearances; it is difficult to assure that there is manageable access to buildings and stages, and all the members have agreed that they'd rather cut back on performances than try to replace Pamela in the group. I think Pam provides the real attraction of the group. The others sing well, but Pam's rich, full alto, her emotional connection with the music and her audience, and her sheer musical knowledge, are assets that are not likely to be found in another amateur singer. And the sense of purpose and fun the group gives Pam is probably what keeps my friend moving at all.

"Black pants or skirts, and red tunics." Pam looks over her half-glasses and raises her eyebrows. "I think Juanita is planning to reveal some cleavage."

"Cleavage? Are you kidding?"

"I think cleavage the size of Juanita's is better off covered," Linda offers.

"Well, you know, first her father made her dress like some religious fanatic, and then her husband wasn't much better. I think she's just now, at the age of 56, feeling like she can do and dress as she darn well pleases." Pam stops talking to count the yarn stitches on her left-hand needle.

Elaine doesn't comment, but smiles and stops quilting for a moment.

Pam describes the fabric she's found to make a new tunic for the performance, and I sink back into my own thoughts. I've known Pam for... twenty-three? twenty-four years now, and Linda for even longer. Elaine is the newbie, since she's 'only' been one of the gang for twelve or fourteen years. Of course, we all knew Billy long before he met Elaine.

I look around the quilt at the women whom I consider my best friends, and realize that Elaine is talking.

"...and I was driving home from town, coming across Buck Mountain, you know?"

"Mmm-huh," Linda murmurs.

"And I saw this little animal just sort of" Elaine stops quilting to slowly lift both her hands, palms up, towards the ceiling "rise up out of the weeds on the side of the road. I just caught sight of it with my peripheral vision, and I realized it was a penguin."

I stare at Elaine, who picks up her needle and goes back to quilting, like she'd just said the sky was blue. So I wait for a punch line. Even though Elaine is not in the habit of making jokes.

"A penguin!" Linda looks up, needle suspended in midair and a slight smile on her face.

"Uh-huh. One of those big ones, you know? Like in that movie about the father penguins that hold their eggs on their feet all winter?"

Now I glance at Pam, who is frowning at Elaine across the quilt. Clearly, Pam isn't in on the joke. Either.

"A penguin?" Linda repeats, this time with incredulity in her voice.

"Yes. He just raised up and waddled across the road right in front of me." Elaine pulls her needle through the quilt and leans forward a little, to position it for the next stitches.

"Wait a minute." Pam puts her knitting in her lap and takes her glasses off her nose. They drop onto her chest, suspended by the shiny black beaded string around her neck. "Are you saying that you saw an actual penguin wandering around on a back road in

Highlands County? In June?"

"Uh-huh." Elaine pulls her needle through the quilt, ziiiiiiip. "Pam, what songs will you be singing, Saturday?"

Pam, her mouth open, turns to me and raises her eyebrows.

"Maybe you just thought it was a penguin. It was probably a..." I pause as I try to imagine what native critter could possibly be mistaken for a large penguin, "cat."

"Cat?" Linda exclaims, as though this was an even more outlandish idea than that of an Antarctic bird wandering the Southern Appalachians.

"Well, a cat could be black and white," I say. Okay, it's pretty lame.

Both Linda and Pam laugh, and I giggle too, but Elaine stitches in silence, apparently unperturbed by the others' disbelief or their laughter.

The next day, Pam calls me to ask, "What did you think about Elaine's vision of a penguin?"

"Vision? I don't think I'd call it a vision."

"Well, what else would you call it? A sighting? I don't think so. I mean, do you really believe there was an actual Emperor penguin strolling across Buck Mountain?"

I laugh, but I am uneasy. Elaine has always been a little "drifty," as Mark says, but we all love Billy and will accept almost anything from her to keep him in our circle. "Well, no. I guess she was just mistaken."

Now it is Pam's turn to laugh, but she does it rather grimly. "C'mon, Norma, she believes she actually saw a penguin. You know she does."

"Well. I guess."

"It's just like that time last year when she claimed she'd talked to her grandmother who's been dead for 20 years. And last fall, when she saw the mountain lion and the black bear walking together."

I can't think of a response to this list.

"Are you there?" Pam asks. She is not known for her patience.

"Yeah. It's just... I don't know, Pam. Elaine has always been a little ditzy."

"Ditzy. Ditzy? Norma, this goes beyond ditzy. Ditzy is when you forget to put the cat out at night. Ditzy is burning the meatloaf. Elaine passed the boundary of ditzy about two incidents ago."

"So, what are you thinking, Pam? Do you want to kick Elaine out of the group?" I will be more than a little disturbed if Pam is suggesting we abandon a friend for less than excellent – compelling - reasons.

"Oh good Lord, of course not. But." Pam's normal mile-a-minute talking speed slows. "I'm really worried, Norma. Aren't you?"

"I guess I hadn't thought much about it." I hate to admit that, up to now, I have just ignored Elaine's eccentricities. I've listened to her descriptions of unlikely events, smiled over them, and not thought of them again.

"Well, think about it now. She's always been a little left of center, but lately she's been 'way off course. Hasn't she? Not all the time, of course, but you know, these things just get stranger and stranger. At least you could chalk up a conversation with her grandmother as the result of a desire to connect with someone she'd loved, but penguins?"

"Just one. A penguin."

"Norma, I'm serious. Or maybe I'm the one who's nuts. Am I?"

Nuts? Had Pam just said the word? Was she trying to say that our friend is seriously unstable? "No, you're right, probably we should all pay more attention to Elaine. She's so quiet, it's easy to forget that she has troubles like the rest of us. Or maybe even more than the rest of us."

"She does not have more troubles than the rest of us."

Too late, I realize it was a little disingenuous to suggest that Elaine's troubles, even if they included being mentally ill, were worse than Pam's MS and sudden widowhood before she'd turned 60.

"Sorry."

"Never mind. I'm just saying, we all do have troubles, Norma. You, me, Linda. Elaine has her share, certainly, but she's not dealing with them in a healthy way."

"So what do you think we should do?" I am completely serious now, not arguing; I am asking Pam what she and Linda and I should do to help someone we all love, who might be – who evidently is - in trouble.

This stumps Pam. It is, after all, what she had called to ask me. "I don't know."

Both of us sit and listen to the faint hum of the phone connection while we think.

Finally I ask, "Do you think Billy realizes what's going on?"

I can hear the sigh in Pam's voice as she answers, "Who knows? Did you ever meet Rachel McAdams?"

I can't help laughing at the memory of Rachel McAdams, the oddball old mountain lady who, among other weirdnesses, spent the last ten or twelve years of her life attending community events wearing precariously positioned, brightly colored and unusually styled wigs that would have done Dolly Parton proud.

"And what does Rachel McAdams have to do with Billy realizing Elaine is having problems?"

"It just goes to show how far people can get out of whack, gradually, and the people watching it happen can be oblivious. Like, they just don't want to see it."

"Oh, people can't ignore it when things get really bad," I say.

"Well, nobody did anything to help poor Rachel until she showed up at a Rescue Squad meeting wearing nothing but her favorite wig and a pair of bedroom slippers! Look Norma, I have to go. But we can't just keep on ignoring this. Somebody has to do something. Don't they?"

"Maybe. Let's see if she says anything at the next meeting. Maybe she's just giving in to her artistic side."

"Yeah. Well. We'll see."

But Spring gave way to summer, and we decided to hold our work meetings on a catch-as-catch-can schedule. There were just too many family obligations, too much mowing and gardening, too many vacations and children home from college, for us to get together every other week. I usually put away my quilting projects in the summer, anyway; heat, humidity and working on heavy layers of cloth and polyester batting have never seemed like a good combination. Life, that old everyday sameness that blends everything into an acceptable backdrop, flowed along.

I did pay special attention to Elaine when I saw her, but I could not put my finger on anything specifically, concretely wrong. I called Elaine occasionally, dropped by her house with extra garden produce or fruit, and saw her at the summer pot-lucks and parties in our community. She seemed, maybe, a little more drifty and distant than usual, but there was nothing alarming. Elaine was just a sweet, off-beat, artistic, woman; the same person Billy married. I began to relax. After all, if there was a real problem, wouldn't Billy turn to Elaine's best friends for help and support?

I was even more reassured when Billy and Elaine hosted a big party for the Fourth, as they had for the past six or seven years. There were all the usual people and food, all the talk and laughter, and if Elaine seemed a little more disorganized than usual, well, she'd told us she was working on a new show for a gallery in Nashville, and was under a fast-approaching deadline. This explained a little extra driftiness. The party wound down when most of the guests piled into vehicles to go in to town, to watch the municipal fireworks show.

As I help Elaine gather drink cans and paper napkins from the front lawn, I ask, "How's everything going?"

"Oh, fine. Do you think people enjoyed the party?"

"Oh yes, of course. Everybody had a great time. The barbequed chicken was perfect."

"Everybody always loves your potato salad. Thanks for making such a big bowl of it."

"Sure." I push another pile of paper plates into the extra-strength trash bag. Without turning towards her, I laugh and ask, "Did you hear Pam telling about that time she and Dave were accosted by a camel?"

"Oh, that's the funniest story, isn't it?"

"Yeah. It is just so weird that they met up with a live camel in a Highlands County cow pasture."

"Uh-huh." Elaine snuggles another beer bottle to the three already cradled in her left arm, then walks to the recycling box on the porch. When she returns to the group of lawn chairs where I've waited, I go back to what I've started. I've decided it's time to put this worry to rest.

"That story about the camel reminded me of the one about you seeing a penguin." I don't turn my body towards Elaine, but watch her carefully from the corner of my eye.

Elaine is folding up lawn chairs. She doesn't react to the comment at all.

I take that as a good sign. "Did you ever decide what it actually was that you saw? That you thought was a penguin?"

Without looking around, Elaine answers, "Oh, it really was a penguin."

I'd started folding an aluminum chair in preparation for carrying it to the porch. I stop in mid-fold, and turn to stare at my friend. In the gathering twilight, Elaine looks completely solid and reassuringly normal: a plump woman in a faded denim skirt and a white blouse, with red, white and blue flipflops on her feet. Elaine always wears her fly-away, blond-mixed-with-grey hair in a knot on top of her head, and with the light from the living room window behind her, I can see how thin tendrils of it have slipped from its holder and seem to float around Elaine's head in the light, moving air of the summer night.

"How do you know?" I ask.

"Hmmm?" Elaine continues to gather the chairs.

"How do you know it was really a penguin?"

"Oh." Elaine keeps working, and keeps her face turned away. "I just do?" There it is, her typical question mark at the end of a declarative sentence.

"You just know?"

"Yes."

"Elaine." I'd never acknowledged them but Pam's worries have been festering in my mind for weeks, and now suddenly feels like the right time to lance that particular boil. I open the chair I'd just folded, and sit down in it. "Elaine, sit down for a minute. I've got to talk to you about this."

Elaine finally looks in my direction. In the dusk, I am barely able to see her face, so I assume she can't read my expression, either. She drags a lawn chair closer and opens it, and sits down facing me.

"What it is you want to talk about?" she asks.

Asked so baldly, I am at a loss. What am I supposed to say, that

I am just wondering whether Elaine is having a joke on her friends with this penguin stuff, or is she completely out of touch with reality? Elaine looks so normal, and honest, and sane, that suggesting otherwise makes me feel crazy.

"Well, I…" I struggle. "It just seems like we never have time for a real talk, these days."

"Oh, I know. Everybody's so busy."

"So, how've you been, really?"

"Oh, I've been okay." It seems to me that Elaine hesitates, slightly, before she adds, "I am awfully tired, lately."

"Really?"

"Yes. But it's probably just because I've haven't been getting a lot of sleep."

I lean back in the plastic chair and slide my feet out of my sandals. Far off, somebody is shooting off fireworks. There are sporadic puffs of colored light on the horizon, and mis-matched pops and thuds. "You been worrying about something?"

"No."

I sense that Elaine is about to tell me something, and suddenly I decide I want the conversation to go in a different direction. "I don't sleep well in the heat," I say.

"Oh, it's not that. I love summer, and being warm. It was so much warmer in Georgia when I was growing up, than it ever is here."

"Poor you." I smile, even though Elaine probably can't see it.

"There's just so much going on around here, any more. In the nights, I mean."

"Stuff going on?"

"Yes. Activity. You know? It keeps me awake, and then I'm sleepy during the day."

I am pretty sure I do not want to hear any more about Elaine's lack of sleep, but I couldn't not ask. "Like what kind of activity?"

"Well, parties? And one night there was a big dance, right there in the cornfield? And Grandmother Covington comes to visit real often."

Oh no. Oh no, oh no, oh no. "These people who party and dance, are they people you know?" I ask quietly, trying to sound normal.

"Oh, it's not people," Elaine looks at me with her eyebrows raised. "It's animals."

I stare at my long-time friend, a middle-aged woman who keeps a decent house and runs errands in the family car and has her own business setting up fantastic, alluring-to-would-be-shoppers scenes in fancy store windows. Imaginative and artistic she undoubtedly is, but she is also grounded and realistic.

At least, she had been.

"Elaine, tell me that again." I want to give her another chance to make it all right.

"That animals had a dance in the cornfield? Well, it must have been a special occasion. They went 'round and 'round in a circle, you know?"

I know I'm staring, but it doesn't matter. Elaine rattles on, like she's relieved to be talking about it.

"It was really very pretty, in the moonlight: the raccoons and the possums, and the foxes were so quick."

Well, at least it was native species, not unicorns and dragons.

"At first I couldn't figure out what was going on. I mean, it just looked weird, all those different kinds of animals together. And then I opened the window and leaned out, and I could hear the music."

I feel a morbid kind of fascination with all of this, all these details. I can't help asking, "What kind of music was it?"

"Very faint. Very faint music, from where I was in the bathroom up there." Elaine gestures towards her house; I can only see the movement of her hand because it is back-lit by the window behind her. That window in the second-floor bathroom has been the subject of much conversation among all the Blevins's friends. It offers the best view in the house. When Elaine and Billy remodeled the old house and put in the upstairs bathroom, Elaine insisted they have a big window - that opened - opposite the commode, because of the view. Later, she'd learned with a mixture of humor and horror that all three of their children had used that window as a late-night exit and entrance to their bedrooms, while Elaine and Billy had thought everyone was sleeping safely at home.

"But it was beautiful. Mostly stringed instruments, and flutes or pipes or something. After that, of course, I kept watch for them. It was so pretty to see, and I thought I might draw some pictures and use them in a window, some time."

"Elaine." I sit up and lean towards her. "Elaine, do you hear what you're saying? Animals dancing in a ring in the cornfield. Are you talking about a work project? Is this some story you've imagined?"

"Imagined? No, I saw it."

"No you didn't, Elaine. It's impossible. Think about it, honey. Come out of your imagination for a minute, and talk to me. Elaine?"

"But I really did see them."

"No, you didn't, not really. It's just like the penguin you imagined –"

"Well, I did see the animals dancing, and I did see the penguin too. It was an Emperor penguin, from Antarctica, and I know that because my grandmother told me."

"Elaine, your grandmother Covington has been dead for twenty years."

"Well, I know that!" Elaine stands up and brushes hair out of her face. "Do you think I'm crazy or something?"

The question hangs between us like a drawn sword, silver and shimmering and almost visible in the dark.

"Oh!" Elaine scoops up two lawn chairs and marches to the porch of her house, where she drops them loudly on the wooden floorboards. Without looking back she opens the screen door and goes inside, letting the door slam behind her.

It was nearly the end of August before the group decided to get together for another work session. It was to be held at my house, and I wondered whether Elaine would come. We'd spoken since the Fourth of July party, but not much. There had been much phoning back and forth among the rest of us, as we'd shared worries and information, and repeated conversations and ideas about what – if anything – should be done to help Elaine.

Pamela called me as soon as she figured I'd had time to contact Elaine, and asked what Elaine had said when I told her about the meeting.

"She said Thursday was fine with her, and that she'd be here,

just like our whole conversation after the party never happened."
Though I'd discussed the scene with both Pam and Linda several
times, no one had been able to come up with a plan for a way to
help Elaine.

"I still think somebody ought to talk to Billy about it. I mean,
what if he really hasn't caught on? He should be taking her to a
counselor or to a doctor or something. She should be on medica-
tion."

"I don't know, Pam. Maybe it's not as bad as all that. Maybe
we're over re-acting. And Mark says we should absolutely not try
to speak to Billy about it. He says, what if Billy does know about it,
and is okay with it? Or doesn't know, and confronts her and some-
thing horrible happens because we dredged it all up?"

"I'm telling you, something needs to be done."

"Okay then, why don't you do it?"

"Oh no, you've known Billy a lot longer than any of the rest of
us have. You should do it."

"Well, I'm not. At least, not yet."

"What are you waiting for, pixies and fairies?"

"No, just the right time."

"Well, I'll see you around one. Maybe the right time is closer
than you think."

After lunch we all gather in my sewing room, in our usual places, each doing her usual work. Either we're all mighty fine liars, or
everybody's decided to give this thing a rest, I think. I am relieved.
Maybe Elaine wasn't as off-centered as I thought, that night after
the party. She was probably thinking about a work project, a story
she could use for a window setting...

Suddenly I tune in to what the others are saying, and I hear, "I
hear your neighbors have been seeing some bears, Norma." Pam
looks at me meaningfully, over her glasses.

"What?" I am totally lost. "Who?"

"I ran into George and Maxine in the grocery store the other
day, and they said they saw a mother bear and her cub in their
blueberries. They've been in there several mornings this week, they
said."

"Yikes. That's a little close to home," I say. George and Maxine Greer moved back to Highlands County after they retired last year; they'd built a home on top of the ridge just above my house.

"Yeah. It's fun to tell visitors that there are bears in the woods here, and kind of fun to see them when you're driving down the road, but in the neighbor's field, on a regular basis? That's too close for comfort." Pam's needles click, adding emphasis to her opinion.

I wish Pam would stop this. It seems cruel to talk about things that are likely to bring unwanted ideas into Elaine's mind. Of course, that is Pam's purpose: not to be cruel, but to bring Elaine's problems out in the open, so she can be helped.

"What about you, Norma? You're right next door. Have you seen any bears?"

I frown at Pam, but Pam just opens her eyes wider and gazes innocently at me. I shoot a glance at Elaine, who is stitching studiously, her entire torso bent over the framed quilt. "No, we haven't seen any right here." Despite myself, I am getting caught up in the superficial conversation about bears. "You know, there was that time Mark met a bear in the road, just around that first corner between here and the store."

"Really? When was that?" Linda sits up, ready, as ever, to hear any kind of story.

"It was about a year ago, I guess. In the fall, when I was making jelly out of the fox grapes we found behind the old Pressy place. Remember? There were so many. Mark was headed to the store to pick up some canning lids for me. He was still kind of shaken up by it, when he told me about it.

"He was driving along, minding his own business. He rounded that curve above the creek, and you know the shoulder is real wide there. So at the moment when the car was pointed straight at that widest grassy place, he realized there was something big and black humped over there, and then, when the car was close to it, it stood up.

"He was in his old car, that green Escort, that sets so low to the ground. When the bear stood up, Mark said it seemed to just tower over him. He stopped the car and was just feet away from that bear, and I think they kind of looked each other in the eye for a few moments. Then the bear went down on all four feet, and moved off."

"Ooooo." Linda says happily. "And that was right here."

"Well, more or less." I pick up my needle and pretend to look for the line I'd been stitching. I was actually looking at Elaine, and remembering that when Mark told me about seeing that bear, he had shivered theatrically and said, "Man, I almost expected that old bear to speak." I am absolutely not going to add that part of the story, not to this group.

Instead, I announce, "You know, we still have a jar or two of that jelly. Would anybody like to try some of it on apple bread? I think it would be a good combination."

When I am passing Pam, on my way to the kitchen, she pulls me into a hug and whispers, "You did a nice job of moving everybody away from the topic of 'Wild Animals I Have Known,' but it's only a delaying tactic. Something's going to happen, sooner or later."

"Maybe not."

"Well, I hope not too, but you just mark my words. And the longer it goes, the worse it'll be."

I tried to forget it, but Pam's prediction weighed like a boulder in my mind. For weeks after that, especially while I was quilting, I remembered Elaine's words from the night of the Fourth, and I analyzed each phrase, trying to be clear about Elaine's meaning without bringing my own feelings into the evaluation. Elaine had said that she saw animals going around in a circle in the corn-field. Maybe there were natural causes for this kind of behaviour. Maybe it was a mating display. I had seen a show on PBS about some birds in Africa that danced before mating, with the males all puffed up and strutting; maybe what Elaine had seen was some-thing similar. In her tiredness and distraction, with her artistic temperament and flighty personality, she'd elaborated on it.

I could easily figure out why Elaine heard music. "Mostly stringed instruments, and flutes or pipes," she'd said. It wouldn't be all that unusual to hear the music of stringed instruments in the night, around here. There are always people getting together, play-ing a few tunes, and in the summer, who knows who camps out and makes music all night? Sound can travel far, on soft summer air.

Elaine had said she saw and talked to her dead grandmother; well, lots of people claimed to see ghosts. Some people make their living as mediums or even ghost chasers.

So I put a lid on my worries, and told myself that all my friends were "doing well" and that all I needed to do was pay attention to where I placed my quilting stitches.

It was Linda who lifted that lid.

The next work session, nearly a month after the session with all the talk of bears, is at my house. We've all agreed that with this mid-September meeting, we will settle back into our twice-a-month schedule. All the college-aged children are back at school, summer guests have come and gone, and most of the gardening and mowing is finished.

"I love the fall," I say, looking out the triple-wide window in my second-story studio. The view from here is never more beautiful than at this time of year, when the leaves of hardwood trees are turning shades of crimson and gold, and the dark pines and hemlocks look sleek and handsome among them. "Thank goodness all the hubbub of summer is over. I must be part bear; I just want to fatten up and go into hibernation – with a lot of quilting projects to keep me occupied, of course."

I've solved the problem of Elaine's eccentricities so well in my own mind that I have no clue what Linda might be frowning about or why she wants me to "come to the kitchen for a minute."

"Do you want me to put on water for tea?" I ask Linda's back as she precedes me out the studio door.

"No. I mean – wait a minute, yeah, go ahead and put the kettle on -- but what I really want is to talk to you in private."

"Oh no. Are things okay with you and Buddy?" Buddy is the current Mr. Linda.

"What? Of course things are fine with me and Buddy."

There's no 'of course' about it, not with all the ex-Mr. Lindas around, I think, and smile. Everybody loves Linda, including me, Pam, Elaine – and most of the men who meet her.

Linda is almost hissing, trying to be quiet and exasperated at the same time. "What I wanted to say was, what made you say that about being a bear?"

"Huh? What did I say?" My comment had been so casual, I'd more or less forgotten having made it.

"You said that you must be part bear, remember?"

"I suppose I did. I didn't mean anything by it; it was just a silly comment on the season. You know, bears, fall, hibernation?"

"Well, I think you'd better explain it to Elaine."

"Elaine?"

"Yes."

"Why? Did I say something that upset her? What am I missing, here?"

"Don't you remember that Elaine has this… thing about animals? Like, penguins?" Linda looks me sternly in the eye. "And bears."

"Oh, no. I thought all that had gone away."

"Well, it has not gone away."

"How do you know?"

"Because she told me."

"She told you what?"

"She told me she's been talking with bears."

My stomach goes into a full-bore cramp. Stress always gets me in the gut first. "When?" I ask.

"When did she tell me, or when was she talking to the bear?" Without looking at me, Linda picks up the kettle and holds it under the faucet, pressing the fancy handle so cold water can run into the pot.

I blink as I try to figure out what Linda has just said. "Both," I finally add.

"Okay. Last week, I needed to go to Asheville to get the stuff to re-paint the guest bedroom. I'm going to marble the walls, you know. Pink, ivory and soft gray. Don't you think that will be pretty?"

"Lovely. So you were going to Asheville."

"Yes. They just don't keep those kinds of paints around here, so I was going to Asheville, and I saw Elaine standing in her yard as I passed, and on a whim I stopped and asked if she wanted to go with me."

"She was just standing there?"

"She was digging up flowers. Dahlias, I think. You know she usually sets that bank along the road in dahlia bulbs."

At this rate, I could've gone to Asheville and back myself, before I hear about what happened to Elaine. But I hold onto my temper and prod, "So you two went to Asheville?"

"Oh. Yes, we went and had a nice day. We ate lunch at Slumgullion's. Do you know that place?"

"Yes. Go on."

"Anyway. While we were eating, Elaine told me about her conversation with the bear."

I had been eager to hear the tale, but now I don't want Linda to tell me any more. I'll just ask about the bedroom, whether she's all finished painting, and --

Linda is now only too eager to continue. "It seems that Elaine was quite taken with your little story about Mark seeing that bear, and she made a point of getting together with the bear – notice I say 'the,' because she did too, like it was the one and only, or the king or something."

Linda pauses to let me comment, but I didn't have anything to say.

"Elaine said the bear – The Bear! – knew who Mark was, and remembered meeting him in the road, and everything. And he said that he knew you, too, and that you have a good spirit or something, and that you have an important role to play."

"In what?" I whisper.

"Hmmm? In what what?"

"A role to play in what?"

"Oh honey, I don't know. I didn't ask. The important thing is that Elaine is really losing it. I mean, I know she was seeing animals before, but at least they were just being animals. I don't know about that grandmother thing, but this, this seems so weird. Doesn't it? Don't you think this is getting serious? And then you said that about being part bear, and I just had to tell you about it right now."

"Oh Lord, Linda, I don't know what to think."

"I don't think we should be thinking. I think it's time to do. Don't you feel that somebody has to do something? Elaine is our friend, and we're losing her. We're losing her because we're not doing anything."

This is uncommonly logical, for Linda. "What should we do?"

"I don't know. Well. To tell you the truth…"

I wait, but Linda seems to have run out of steam until she sighs and says, "I'll tell you what. You and Pam stay until after Linda leaves this afternoon, and we'll talk it out. Maybe together we can figure out something."

We work through the afternoon, and if conversation is unusually scarce or strained, Elaine does not seem to notice. She gathers her things and leaves "in time to fix supper," and Pam, Linda and I take seats close together. After Linda re-tells her account of the trip to Asheville, (with a commendable lack of dramatic additions, I notice) Pam bounces her rubber-tipped cane on the floor and says, "We should have taken steps months ago."

"What were we supposed to do?" I had agonized over this time and again and then had put it out of my mind. There was just nothing to be done!

Linda says, "You know, Elaine is an adult and appears – to people who don't know her well - to be perfectly capable. We couldn't make anything happen, no matter what we did. Except ruin our friendship."

We sit in silence for two or three whole minutes. Then Pam says, "You're right, Linda. There's not much we can do, directly. The only thing we can do is make sure the person who can do something directly, is aware of the need for action. Somebody's got to talk to Billy."

Nobody looks at me, but I say to both of their bowed heads, "Please don't make me do this."

"I know you don't want to."

"And Mark insists that I shouldn't meddle –"

"Well, don't you agree that this has gone beyond the point of letting it slide?" Pam looks me in the eye and doesn't let me turn away. "Yes or no?"

I refuse to answer, but my silence is as good as a verbal "yes."

Pam continues, more gently, "You know him best, Norma. You and Billy have been friends for years longer than we've known him. He probably trusts you most, and Elaine trusts you."

"Besides, " Linda inserts, "you can explain things better than any of us."

"Maybe me knowing him better means you two don't understand how sensitive Billy is about some things... Maybe it means that he'll feel worse that it comes from me, like someone he trusts most is betraying him."

Again, we fall into a long silence. The last bit of the day's sunlight shoots through the big window and lands on my hands clenched together in my lap; in only a few moments, it fades away. The unshadowed light between sunset and dark bathes my house and us, and I think that light is one reason I've always loved this place and my special room. I've always felt it was a kind of sweet magic, warm and illuminating.

"Honey," Linda whispers, "do you want us to go with you?"

I take a deep breath. "No," I say. "I think it would be best coming from me alone."

It was even worse than I'd thought it would be. Halfway through the conversation I thought that Billy was unreasonably upset, and then I wondered how much would have been "reasonable?" If someone you'd known and trusted for years came to you and said she thought the love of your life, the mother of your children, was crazy and you should be helping her, what would be a "reasonable" response? But I realized that Billy was more-than-upset because at some level, he'd known something was wrong. He was bound to have had some sense that his wife of fifteen years was slipping away. Maybe he hadn't wanted to admit it, or maybe he'd been afraid of what was causing it. Maybe he had reasons for his too-strong reaction to his wife's mental illness, that were even more unpleasant? But by the end of our talk, he seemed to have calmed down. He'd agreed to consider what I'd said. I hoped he would hold on to my last request: to believe that if something was wrong, even seriously wrong, with Elaine's thinking, there would be treatments. There would be help. "Something wrong" does not equal "something permanent," I'd said, unless those who love Elaine allowed it to be that way.

I know that Pam and Linda are worrying and waiting, but it takes me a couple of days to gather my wits so I can tell them about my conversation with Billy. Eventually, I call each of them and explain that although Billy had tried to reject what I'd said, in the end he'd agreed to consider it and make his own assessment. They do not ask me for details, and I am glad. I am also glad for their support. They really are good friends. They really are acting with love.

None of us hears from either Elaine or Billy.

A week drags by, and then another. Pam, Linda and I agree to have a work meeting. It's been almost a month since the last meeting. We debate whether to contact Elaine and invite her to join us, a debate that continues after we are seated around the quilting frames in my sewing room.

"'Invite?' We could beg," Linda says.

"We have to respect the fact that she may not want to be with us any more," I point out.

"Do we even know she's at home now?" Pam asks. "You know, she could be in the hospital…"

A deep silence threatens to completely vacuum out the room, until I say, "I don't know. I haven't heard a word from them. But I think it's time we call."

"You mean, right now?" Linda is hesitant, but Pam pulls a cell phone from her bag, producing it almost instantly.

"Wow, that was fast," I mutter.

Pam answers, "I've had it in my hand three times, and each time I've put it back. I'm such a coward."

"I'm not sure you'll get a signal, here," I begin, when the old-fashioned ring of the landline phone interrupts. I stand and go to the phone on the bookshelf on the west wall. Linda and Pam can hear my end of the conversation, and after the first words, they listen avidly.

"Hello?" I say. "Billy. We were just –"

"What? What? When?"

"Of course. Of course, we'll be right there. Oh Billy – "

But I realize I am talking to a severed connection, and slowly replace the receiver in its cradle. I turn and walk back to my friends, who wait silently, knowing something is wrong. Before they can ask, I tell them, "We need to go to Elaine's house. Billy said... Billy said she's disappeared."

We arrive within minutes. The sheriff's car is parked in front of Billy and Elaine's house, and when we go in – without knocking, with Pam, in her hurry having forgotten her cane, leaning uncharacteristically and heavily on my arm – a deputy dressed in brown and khaki is standing near the door.

Billy rushes towards towards us, and he grabs my arm just above the elbow. "Would you please tell him what you told me, about Elaine? They don't believe me, they won't do a thing."

"Now Mr. Blevins, you know we want to help." The deputy speaks in a tone that is carefully modulated to promote calm but also betrays his irritation. You couldn't come up with a tone of voice more perfectly geared to get on my nerves, not if you practiced for a hundred years, I think. "But an adult can't be listed as missing until 36 hours have passed since the initial report was filed." He looked at us for the first time. "Unless there are complicating circumstances such as health issues or a record of mental instability. Would you identify yourself, please?"

Billy cut in. "This is Norma, Elaine's friend that I was telling you about. She figured out something was wrong with Elaine. She told me – Here, Norma, you tell him. Tell him we have to start a search."

"Well, I, I... I don't know where to start."

"Just tell him what you told me!" Billy yells. "You seemed to have plenty to say the other day! Just tell him, so we can find her."

"What's happened, Billy?" Linda cries. "Where's Elaine?"

"I wish I knew!" Billy sounds wild.

The deputy steps closer and speaks even more quietly. "People, let's get organized and calm down a little. It doesn't help if we lose control of ourselves. Ma'm?" he says, looking at Linda, "do you think you could make some coffee? I don't think Mr. Blevins has had anything to eat today."

"Oh. Sure." Linda moves away from the others, and the deputy deftly takes Pam's arm and guides her to the couch.

"Why don't you sit here. What is your name, ma'm?"

"Pamela Hatcher."

"Ms Hatcher, are you a friend of the Blevins's?"

"Yes. Yes, Elaine, Norma, Linda and I are long-time friends."

The deputy turns to look at me. "You're Norma?" The drawn-out final syllable is an inquiry, and I answer,

"Merritt. Norma Merritt."

"Okay, Ms Merritt, why don't you sit beside your friend, and Mr. Blevins, you sit over here. I'll pull this chair in a little closer and now we can start to get this story straight."

The deputy takes out a small, narrow notebook and pulls a pen from his shirt pocket. He looks at me and asks, "Now Ms Merritt, how long have you known Mrs. Blevins?"

I turn slightly, to look at Billy like maybe I need to see him to confirm what I am about to say. "We met Elaine when Billy and she started dating. That would have been… sixteen years ago?"

"Seventeen," Billy corrects.

The deputy makes a notation in his little book. "Okay. Long-time friends, would you say?"

"Yes. We live in the same neighborhood, raised our children together. For the past eight or ten years, we've had this little group that meets to work on projects together. Just, you know, combining hand work and visiting."

"Have you noticed anything unusual about Mrs. Blevins's behaviour lately?"

I look at Billy; I want him to feel how awful I feel, how sorry I am, how much I want to hear what's happened. He gazes back at me, hard-eyed and hot. "Yes. We've all realized Elaine was… not herself."

"What do you mean, 'not herself'?"

"She…" I cannot bring myself to say these things about Billy's wife, in front of Billy.

He takes the initiative. "Just tell him," he barks.

"Elaine told us that she was seeing things that, that probably weren't there."

The deputy cocks his head. "Could you explain that?"

"She thought she'd seen her grandmother, and a penguin, and a group of animals, dancing." My voice sinks, softer and slower as I recite the list. It sounds awful, said like this.

"Where is Mrs. Belvins's grandmother?"

"She's dead," Billy says, with a voice that sounds like he's been clearing his throat with ground glass. "Been dead since a month after we got married."

The deputy makes another note. "When did this behaviour start?"

"Well, we aren't sure."

"I didn't know anything about it until two weeks ago," Billy croaks. "That's when these ladies saw fit to inform me."

Neither Pam nor I is inclined to defend herself against this accusation.

The deputy turns to Billy. "You, yourself, didn't notice anything unusual was going on?"

A deep flush rises up Billy's neck, but he says steadily enough, "No."

Looking back at his notes, the deputy continues, "What happened after they told you Mrs. Blevins was seeing things?"

Pam and I both wince when the deputy states it so bluntly, but we also lean forward to hear Billy's answer. What had happened after I had talked to him about Elaine?

"Well," he begins, and he looks at some point beyond the arm of the couch, "for a couple of days, I just... I just thought about it. I didn't believe it. I mean, Norma was saying that my wife was... that she was crazy." Billy shifts his gaze to the deputy's face. "That couldn't be right. Elaine wasn't acting crazy, and she looked the same as always. She was, she was a wife to me, and was working on projects and doing things like always. How could there be anything wrong?"

If he is waiting for some show of understanding, he doesn't get it from the deputy. Billy looks down at his hands that are clenched in his lap. "So I decided I would just ask her. The first chance to sit down together and talk was last night. I asked her if she'd been feeling all right, and she said yes. And I asked her if she'd had a quarrel with her friends." Billy raises his head and looks, angry and hurt, at Pam and me. "And she said no, of course not. We talked about other stuff, you know, like what she was working on and when she'd talked to her parents. And then I asked her if she'd seen any unusual animals around the place lately."

We stare at Billy. The deputy watches him intently. In the kitchen doorway, Linda stands with a loaded tray in her hands.

"She said no, not really. And I was so relieved. But she added that if I was interested in unusual animals, I should come to the dance with her tomorrow night. That would be tonight, I guess."

"What dance?" the deputy asks.

"That's what I said. 'What dance?' Why, the animals' dance, she said. In the corn field. Now that the dance floor's been cleared, they'll have a big dance."

"The dance floor's been cleared?" the deputy wonders.

"I think..." Billy watches his hands as they, apparently of their own volition, twist and turn. "I think she meant that the field had been harvested. Sam and his brother cut the corn off that field yesterday."

Billy suddenly jerks himself upright. "And then we had a big argument," he says. How awful it is to have to tell this kind of thing to a stranger, someone who doesn't know that you have a good marriage, that you're not just acting like a married person, but are truly and deeply married, committed. Someone who might not know that any argument you have is just clearing the air, not clearing the deck. Billy stands, paces back and forth across the room. "I was yelling at her to stop this craziness, and she was yelling back that it was not crazy, that the animals would come and dance. She said her grandmother had promised her that it would be a good time, that it was okay to go. Her grandmother. She's been talking to her grandmother, and she thinks her grandmother's been answering."

The deputy ignores Billy's pacing. He's making more notes in the little notebook, and it seems to me that when he speaks again, the tone of the deputy's voice is different from before. It is cooler, more crisp, but still very, very calm. "Would you say that your argument with your wife was violent?" he asks.

"What?"

"Now you stop right there," Pam interrupts. "I know what you're getting at, and you are wrong. Maybe you have to suspect the husband first, but there is absolutely no way —"

The deputy blusters and Linda brings in the tray and tries to get everyone to settle down and drink coffee, and the whole gathering disintegrates. An hour later, the deputy leaves and Pam,

Linda, Billy and I are sitting around the Blevins's kitchen table. We'd been assured by the deputy that extra patrols in the area and across the county would be notified to watch for a woman fitting Elaine's description, and if another couple of days pass and Elaine still hasn't shown up, a full-scale search will be launched. It seemed to be his opinion that, following their quarrel, Elaine had gone off on her own to calm down or to teach her husband a little lesson.

We know better. Elaine would never have left to punish Billy, and if she'd needed to "cool off," an hour's walk would have done it. We try to think of any place Elaine would have gone; in which direction she might have walked.

"And after you and Elaine argued, she just walked away?" I ask Billy, for the third or fourth time.

He stares out the window without answering.

"Which way did she go?" Pam asks. "How far have you looked in that direction? Maybe she got further than you think."

"We could go look again," I say, and stand up. "Linda and I can go. Maybe women would go in a different route from the one a man would take. Pam, you stay here and call Linda's cell if Elaine shows up, okay?"

"She didn't walk away." Billy's voice is almost too soft to hear, but I catch a word or two.

"What?" I turn back, my hand already on the back door handle.

Billy hunches his shoulders and turns his face away. "Elaine didn't walk away from our argument. I did."

I go back to the table and sit down. "Where is Elaine, Billy?" I ask.

"I don't know. I don't know because I walked away. I was the one who walked out. She was sitting right here, the last time I saw her."

"Why didn't you tell the deputy the truth?" Pam was never one to avoid asking straightforward questions.

"I thought it made me look bad. Like I couldn't handle her being sick. And I wanted them to start looking for her right now, and I thought… Oh God, I'm not sure what I thought, now."

"Billy." Pam leans forward and uses the tone of a parent to a child who has stretched her patience to the breaking point. "Where was Elaine, the last time you saw her?"

"Right," Billy pounds his fist on the tabletop, "here. She was right…" He stops and swallows, "here. Oh God, she was right here and I left her."

I take one of Billy's hands in mine. "It's all right, Billy. Elaine knows how much you care for her."

"She needed me. And I was so scared, all I did was yell at her."

"It's all right. It's going to be all right."

We search all afternoon, and into the night. We take flash-lights and drive two of our cars to the edge of the cornfield. For long hours we patrol around the edges of the field, and we keep the cars' engines idling, lights on, illuminating the flat, stubbled ground. We wonder if – we hope that – Elaine will come back to the field, for the animals' dance. But neither Elaine nor any animal comes near.

As time passes, Billy grows more distraught, more sure that something terrible has happened to his wife. "She would have come back," he says, over and over. "Elaine would have come back if she could. I know she would have come back."

Finally, I convince Billy to lie down and wait for daylight before continuing the search. I send Pam home to rest, aware that the symptoms of her illness are growing more and more noticeable as she tires. Mark goes back to our house, to gather supplies he thinks might be useful during the next day's search. Linda and I sit at the kitchen table, cups of herbal tea gradually cooling in front of us. Finally, I ask the question that has been twisting my guts into a knot. "Linda. Is this our fault?"

Linda closes her eyes and leans her forehead on one hand. After a moment, she answers softly, "Yes. I think it is."

I put my head down on my crossed arms. "I know. I never meant for this to happen."

"We all only wanted to help. We were doing the best we could think of. But if we hadn't pushed Billy, Elaine wouldn't have run away."

My head jerks up. "We don't know for sure that she's run away!"

Linda looks steadily into my eyes. "What do you think hap-pened?"

I close my eyes because I can't bear to see what's in Linda's. "Where do you think she can have gone?"

"I don't know."

"What if she's lying somewhere in the dark, hurt?"

"Norma."

"What if someone took her, abducted her while she's not thinking clearly?"

"Norma! That's enough."

I scrub at my face with my bare hands. "I'd give a hundred dollars for a hot shower."

"Okay, go take one."

I look at my friend, feeling blurred with fatigue.

"Go on," Linda says. "It's nearly dawn. I'll stay here, and we'll start again when Buddy and Mark get back. You'll be able to help more, after a shower."

All of that was more than a year ago. We searched, and more of the neighbors joined in, and finally the police from the state, and even other localities across the whole United States, tried to find our lost friend. But no one did. After a few weeks, the excitement fizzled out and all the people who were not closely connected to Billy and Elaine Blevins went back to their normal lives. Reporters stopped calling, church ladies stopped bringing casseroles and cakes, and all but a few of the weirdos and crazies who had fixated on this story stopped hanging around and trying to catch a glimpse Billy's and Elaine's children.

Linda calls and asks if she can come over for a few minutes. I answer her knock reluctantly, but find, when I look at my old friend's face, that I am glad to see her, after all. I ask Linda to come in, and we go automatically to my sewing room, where I sit down at the big quilting frames and pick up my needle.

"This is a beautiful quilt," Linda says, rubbing her fingers lightly over the top, pieced in shades of crimson, rust, and burgundy. "What's this pattern called?"

"Storm at Sea."

"All these reds... don't look particularly ocean-y."

"Hmm."

Linda watches me stitching for a few seconds, and then asks,

"Would it be okay if I quilted a little?"

I look up and study her face, then release a long-held breath. "Sure. I'll get another pair of scissors, and a thimble."

The two of us quilt in silence for fifteen minutes, and what had seemed strained slowly settles into peace. After twenty minutes, I see that my stitches have begun to even out; the lines of quilting run straight and true across the blocks. Nearly half an hour passes before Linda asks, "Have you seen Pam lately?"

I do not look up when I answer, "Not since the memorial."

We work for a few minutes more, until Linda pulls a knot to rest between the quilt layers, re-threads her needle, and pushes the point of the needle into the fabric. She knows this is the way I like to leave a quilt-in-progress, everything ready to begin the next session. "Norma," she says quietly, "I came to tell you something."

"Linda," I hurry to interrupt, "please don't."

"But I –"

"I really don't want to talk about it. Please." I keep my head averted, eyes on my quilting.

"Norma, I'm leaving."

My hands fall into stillness, and I look up. "Oh," is all I can say.

"I mean, Buddy and I are leaving Highlands County. We're moving to Asheville."

"Oh." Very quietly.

"Before I go, I have to tell you something, something about Elaine."

"Please don't. I've been trying to put it all behind me."

"I know. So have I, but it's been harder for me."

"Harder for you? You weren't the one who talked Billy into confronting her."

"No."

"I am the most to blame. I have the most to answer for."

"No."

"Yes. Be honest." My voice sounds hard; it is ragged with guilt.

"But I…" Linda swallows, closes her eyes. "I'm the last one who saw her. I saw her that morning, and I didn't stop her."

A heartbeat of time passes, then another. "You what?" I whisper.

Now Linda speaks quickly, in a rush to get it all out. "Do you remember that morning, it was nearly dawn and you were so tired and everybody else had gone home or was asleep? Even Billy was asleep, for a little while."

"I remember."

"And you went up to take a shower, and I told you I'd keep watch. And I did, and in fact, I realized it was starting to get light, and I thought I'd go out on the porch and look, just look all around, just in case. You know?"

Linda pauses, but I have nothing to say.

"It was cold. Early October." Linda pauses for a moment, and says in an undertone, "Almost exactly a year ago." Then she shakes her head and goes on, louder. "A big frost had fallen, and the sun was just behind the ridge when I stepped outside, and then, suddenly, the first rays shot across Elaine and Billy's front yard and the frost all turned to glitter. It was so pretty. Even upset as I was I couldn't help but love it all, the mountains and the sharp air and the white and silver frost." Linda closes her eyes for a moment.

"And then I noticed that the frost had been marked. There were places where the grass had been bent, tracks, coming from around the east corner of Elaine's house, crossing the front yard and the road. You could see tracks in the frost, when the light was laid straight across it like that. I kept following those tracks with my eyes, across the yard and the road and into the corn field."

I take a sudden, deep breath – it sounds so loud, in that pretty room where we've spent so much time -- but I do not speak. Linda looks straight into my eyes, and continues as if she is describing something that is happening in there with us. "It was just getting light, and at first I wasn't sure. I stepped off the porch, and then took a few steps more." I see Linda's hands making the motions of pulling a sweater across her chest, although she isn't wearing a sweater and it is perfectly warm in my sewing room. "And then I ran to the field."

"Why didn't you tell somebody?" I cry. "Why didn't you ever tell anybody?"

"Elaine wasn't alone," Linda says quietly. "I called her name, but she didn't turn around. I got closer, and I could hear her voice. She sounded so happy." Tears are crawling slowly down Linda's cheeks. "She had her hand on the shoulder of a bear and she was laughing as they walked away together."

Linda covers her face with both her hands and sits for a minute, her shoulders shaking, childlike sobs muffled behind her hands. When the sobs finally ease, she wipes her cheeks with her hands and her nose with her sleeve. "How could I tell anyone that?" she says. "Everyone would have thought I was crazy."

"What happened?" I am shouting at her now, my best friend, who is in such hurt. I yell, "What did you do? What happened to Elaine?"

"I didn't know what to do. Was I hallucinating? What if I frightened that bear and it attacked her, or me? Finally... They were moving away, leaving me behind at the edge of the corn field, in the cold dawn light. Finally, I called, 'Elaine? Elaine?'

"She hesitated. She stopped for one moment. But she never turned her head, and finally she just leaned over against that bear – its shoulder was waist-high on her – and put both her arms around its neck, and pushed her face into its fur. Then they walked on together."

"Linda," I whisper. "Where did they go?"

Linda stands up, and picks up her purse. She is not looking at my face now, when she says. "I do not know. I was crying. I put my hands over my eyes, and when I took them down, Elaine and the bear were gone. They were just... gone." She turns and walks to the door.

When her hand is on the knob, I ask, "Why did you tell me this now?"

Linda is still for a moment, indecision or sorrow or some other emotion pulling every line in her body downward. Then she pulls the door open and steps into the hall, facing the front door. Without looking at me, she says, "Yesterday, on my way home from town, I saw a penguin on Buck Mountain."

Deborah Tilson Clark is a native of Southwest Virginia. She lives in Grayson County, in a log house on the banks of Guffy Creek, with her husband and a Siamese cat. She has been a daughter, a wife, a mother, and a friend; she has worked as (among other things) a craftsmaker, store keeper, park naturalist, house cleaner, newspaper writer, and teacher. She first submitted a story to a publisher when she was eight yeas old. It did not sell, but she was undeterred.

Made in the USA
Columbia, SC
25 April 2019